CAT KILLER: NANCY JAMES

Jovan Taylor

13HORROR.COM BOOKS
An imprint of
DIZZY EMU PUBLISHING
1714 N McCadden Place, Hollywood, Los Angeles 90028
dizzyemupublishing.com

Cat Killer: Nancy James
Jovan Taylor

First published in the United States
in 2022 by 13Horror.com Books/Dizzy Emu Publishing

CAT KILLER: NANCY JAMES

Jovan Taylor

OVER BLACK--

EXT. NEIGHBORHOOD STREET - NIGHT

A small town American HOME on a small town street. The grass
is nicely mowed, and there are a couple of flower pots by the
front door. The welcome mat is simple yet homey.

We DEIFT UP towards a warm, lighted yellow window, on the
second floor. There is a young girl sitting on her bed who
reaches over and turns off her light.

INT. HOUSE - AMANDA'S ROOM - NIGHT

The CAMERA PULLS BACK to reveal AMANDA Taylor, 16: alone in
her bedroom scrolling through her phone while laying down on
her bed. Her room is white or a light color with a couple of
posters on the wall, a light green bedspread, a laptop on her
desk that's closed, a backpack and sweater on the back of a
chair, and a pair of shoes spray on the floor. At the corner
of her room, on an extra chair, she has a teddy bear facing
her bed. She has a few extra teddy bears on the foot of her
bed, and on her desk is an agenda notebook closed with a pen
sitting on top.

                    AMANDA
               (scoffs)
          Oh my God! she did not post that!
          You bitch!

Amanda gets a text message from an unknown number, she swipes
the message off her screen and continues scrolling through
her phone when she gets another message. Amanda groans in
annoyance as she sits up and opens the message.

                    AMANDA (CONT'D)
          What do you want?

Amanda reads the message aloud.

                    AMANDA (CONT'D)
          Hey, princess!
               (realizing who it is)
          Chad?

She replies to the message. On the screen it reads, "Is this
Chad?" She goes back to scrolling through her phone after
sending the message.

                    AMANDA (CONT'D)
          Oh! That looks cute!

Amanda gets a response from the unknown number saying "Yea,
it's me haha! Watchu doing?" Amanda rolls her eyes and laughs
as she starts typing but hears a noise a noise coming from
the hallway. She gets out of bed.

                    AMANDA (CONT'D)
               (annoyed)
          Ugh! He better be sleep.

Amanda tosses her phone on the bed and walks towards her door
and leaves her room.

AMANDA'S HOUSE - HALLWAY

Amanda walks towards her little brothers bedroom, she opens
the door and peeks her head inside and sees him asleep. She
closes the door and heads downstairs into the kitchen. On the
way to the kitchen there is a hall closet and a mirror close
to the front door.

AMANDA'S HOUSE - KITCHEN

Amanda walks downstairs into the kitchen and opens fridge,
grabbing a bottle of water. She turns her head and notices
the back door slightly open. She puts her water bottle on the
counter as she slowly walks towards the back door leaving the
fridge wide open, she looks through the window into the
backyard, as she shuts and locks the door.

                    AMANDA
          That was odd..

She walks back to close the fridge and sees her little
brother DAVID Taylor, 8: standing in front of her. Amanda
jumps as she grabs her chest.

                    AMANDA
          God damn it, David! Why are you
          up?!

                    DAVID
          I want some water.

                    AMANDA
          No, you'll piss your bed and I'm
          not gonna change your sheets. Go
          back to bed.

                    DAVID
          But Amanda-

Amanda turns David around as she pushes him back towards the
stairs and forces him to go back upstairs.

                    AMANDA
          No "buts" David! Don't make me call
          mom and dad.

David stomps as he returns upstairs into his room, while
Amanda shakes her head as she grabs her water bottle and goes
back to her room.

AMANDA'S HOUSE - AMANDA'S ROOM

Amanda returns to her room she takes another sip of her water
and puts it on her desk, then jumps onto her bed. She grabs
her phone and finishes typing her message "Watching my
brother. Did you get a new number?" She saves the number as
"Chad" and sends the text. Then she gets a phone call from
Chad. Amanda looks puzzled but still answers the call.

                    AMANDA
          Yea?

Chad can be heard through the phone playing a video game.

                    CHAD
               (phone)
          Boom, bitch! Hey, baby!

Amanda realizes Chad is playing is game in the background.

                    AMANDA
          Did you really call me while your
          gaming?

                    CHAD
               (phone)
          I wanted to hear your voice! It
          gives me good luck!
               (yelling at his game)
          FUCKING SHOOT HIM!! WHAT ARE YOU
          DOING?!

Amanda laughs as she listens to Chad get mad at his game.

                    AMANDA
          You take those game way to serious
          hah.

                    CHAD
               (phone)
          Not even, haha.

Amanda and Chad share a quick laugh, then she hears a noise from the hallway again.

                    AMANDA
          Ugh, hold on!

Amanda puts her phone on her dresser as she gets out of bed and goes to check on her brother again.

AMANDA'S HOUSE - HALLWAY

Amanda walks down the hall to her brother's room and opens the door seeing him under the covers. She rolls her eyes.

                    AMANDA
          You better go to sleep David!

Amanda leaves closing the door and returning to her room.

AMANDA'S HOUSE - AMANDA'S ROOM

Amanda returns to her room and jumps on her bed as she reaches for her phone.

                    AMANDA
          You still there?!

                    CHAD
              (phone)
          Yea, just starting my next match.
          What happened?

                    AMANDA
          Davids begin a brat again.

                    CHAD
              (phone)
          You're babysitting tonight? Why
          didn't you tell me, I would've came
          over.

Amanda expresses a confused expression.

                    AMANDA
          What are talking about? I told you
          earlier I was babysitting.

                    CHAD
              (phone)
          No, you didn't baby.

                    AMANDA
          I just texted you not too long ago
          saying "I'm watching David"
          remember? You texted me said "Hey,
          Princess".

                    CHAD
               (phone)
          Baby, I didn't text you....I'm just
          now getting home from practice.

                    AMANDA
          What do you-

Amanda hears more noise coming from the hallway, as if
someone is going down stairs. She sits up on her bed
listening with a worried expression on her face. She gets
another message from Chad saying "Haha, you're so easy
Amanda". Her eyes widen as she begins to freak out. She
quickly deletes tat as "Chad" and leaves it marked as
"Unknown"

                    CHAD
               (phone)
          Amanda? Amanda, are you okay!

                    AMANDA
               (scares)
          Chad if you're trying to scare me
          it's not funny! knock it off!

                    CHAD
               (phone)
          I'm not doing anything!

She gets another text saying "Hang up the phone or your
little brother dies!". She covers her mouth trying not to
scream.

                    CHAD
               (phone/worried)
          Amanda!?

                    AMANDA
               (terrified)
          I-I I gotta go, Chad!

                    CHAD
               (phone)
          What? Amanda no wai-

Amanda hangs the phone up on Chad cutting him off mid sentence, as she gets out of her bed and rushes toward her door about to open it, when she gets a text message with a picture of her living room downstairs.

                    AMANDA
               (terrified)
          That's my living room!!

Another message comes through saying "I'm downstairs. You have a beautiful house. I particularly like this mirror..." Amanda backs away from her door shaking in fear. she shakes her head in denial.

                    AMANDA
               (through tears)
          This isn't happening! This isn't
          real!

Amanda begins to cry when she gets another text "Stop crying you brat! I hate whining children". Amanda breakdown crying as she replies to the number "How do you know what I'm doing?!". Another message comes through this time it's a video of Amanda getting out of bed and walking toward the door.

Her eyes widen in pure terror as she covers my mouth as she continues to cry. "What do you want from me" Amanda replies as she falls to her knees in tears. A message comes through "To see what your insides look like!" Amanda drops her phone completely mortified.

EXT. AMANDA'S HOUSE - NIGHT

A blue sedan pulls up onto the street right in front of Amanda's house, turns the engine off and the lights turn off.

INT. AMANDA'S HOUSE - AMANDA'S ROOM

Amanda gets another video message from the unknown number of a lady in a blue car pumping gas. Amanda wipes her tears and showing her exasperated stress

                    AMANDA
               (through tears)
          Why are you showing me this?!

The unknown number sends another message "There's a blue car outside your house. The person driving that is a FBI agent who's been tracking me for the last 6 months" Amanda picks up her phone and replies back "Why are you telling me this?!" The unknown number responds "I like a good hunt!

It makes the kill more fun, haha!" Amanda tries to call 911,
but gets another message "Call 911 and I'll kill your
brother".

                    AMANDA
               (crying)
          How are you watching me?!?

She gets a response "Remember that bear you picked up in
front of your house coming home from school?". Amanda freezes
with fear as she slowly turns her head at the teddy bear in
the corner of her room, she gets up and walks over to it. She
picks it up and stares at it.

                    AMANDA
               (terrified)
          No...

The number responds "That's my nanny bear. I've been watching
you for weeks, I've seen EVERYTHING Amanda, ha!" Amanda reads
the message and throws the bear on the ground in a rage and
flips it off, as she grabs her blanket and throws it over the
bear. she gets another text "I'm gonna cut that finger off
and leave it for your parents to find you little bitch!"

Amanda runs over to her window and sees the blue sedan parked
outside. She tries to get the drivers attention by waving.
The driver flashes their headlights letting her know she sees
her. Amanda gets another text "Think you can make it to the
car with your brother? Good luck! You'll die before you reach
the front door". Amanda screams at the top of her lungs as
she races out of her room into the hallway, to get her
brothers room a fast as she can.

INT. AMANDA'S HOUSE - DAVID'S ROOM - NIGHT

Amanda pushes the door and tries to walk her brother.

                    AMANDA
          David! David!

She looks back over her shoulder into the hallway to see if
anyone is coming up the stairs, as she continues to try as
wake up David. She stares shaking him uncontrollably but then
realizes he's not waking up. Instead she throws her arms in
frustration.

                    AMANDA
               (sacred)
          God damn it, David! Wake the fuck
          up!

Amanda picks up David and throws him over her shoulder so can run more quickly. She runs to the stairs. Quickly, but carefully, she runs downstairs carrying her brother, she almost trips on the last step but catches herself in time. She looks around making sure the person from the unknown number is nowhere to be found. She makes a run for the front door, she looks at the mirror for a split second before she bolts out the front door. Amanda waves her free hand at the blue sedan and runs as fast as she can right up to the back door. Amanda fumbles with the door handle for a second and then she quickly yanks it open.

INT. BLUE CAR - OUTSIDE AMANDA'S HOUSE

Amanda sets her brother on the other side of the seat and gets into the car, looking forward and then quickly shutting the door. She then leans over towards her brother to put his seatbelt on. Then she realizes, he still isn't waking up and wait...is he breathing? She begins shaking in terror a she realizes her brother is dead. She glances and then her attention quickly shifts to the rear-view mirror as she realizes that the person in the front seat is staring at her creepily. That woman staring at her is the alleged FBI agent, who is actually NANCY James, 30: wearing an FBI jacket, she keeps facing forward only looking at them through the mirror with a creepy smile.

                    NANCY
          What's wrong?

Amanda is panicking and still terrified as she tries to explain what happened but can ya seem to make out words.

                    AMANDA
               (terrified)
          S-someone's in my house...and
          they're trying to kill us!

Amanda reaches over to check David and feels something wet on her hand. She pulls her hand back and sees it's blood, she lifts her brothers neck, and sees it's been cut. She lets go of his head as she scoots back towards the door crying, as she realizes her brother's neck was sliced.

                    AMANDA
               (crying)
          David...I'm so sorry....I'm
          sorry...

                    NANCY
          Don't worry Amanda, you'll join him
          soon.

Amanda's heart drops to her stomach as her eyes widen and her tears stop momentarily. She turns her heads towards the driver.

                    AMANDA
               (terrified)
          How do you know my name...

Nancy turns around and smiles at Amanda.

                    NANCY
          Tsk. Tsk. Tsk. You were no fun at
          all.

Amanda tries to open the door but they're on child safety locks. She starts banging on the window screaming for help. Nancy rolls her eyes.

                    NANCY
          Stop crying you brat!

                    AMANDA
               (terrified)
          Why are you doing this?!

Nancy leans more towards the back of the with a psychotic smile on her face as she looks Amanda in the eyes.

Nancy stab Amanda in the stomach with her knife and smiles as she pushes it in deeper. Amanda looks down at the knife as blood starts to drip from her mouth, she tries to push Nancy's hand back , but Nancy grabs her hand and breaks Amanda's middle finger.

                    AMANDA
               (slowly dying)
          Aha...please..

Nancy starts mocking Amanda.

                    NANCY
          Aww, sweetheart it's too late for
          "please".

Nancy pulls the knife out and stabs Amanda in her chest, and watches as Amanda slowly bleeds out and dies in the backseat of the stolen car. Her lifeless body sliding over and landing her David's body.

                    NANCY
          Aw, that's so cute! haha-aha! such
          a shame, all you had to do was stay
          in the house Amanda.

Nancy starts the car and drives off through the neighborhood
playing the song "Smooth Criminal" as WE PULL BACK and get a
wide shot of the neighborhood.

INT. LILY'S HOUSE - ZOEY'S ROOM - MORNING

Zooey is asleep under her covers in her twin size bed next to
her desk. Her room is filled with posters of her favorite boy
bands and movies. She has two of her favorite movies on top
of her tv, very similar to Amanda's bedroom. She has a bunch
of stuffed animals on her nightstand and an agenda book from
school. She has a picture of her and her dad in the desk, her
alarm on her phone goes off, she sticks her arm out to grab
her phone on her desk but can't get it. It falls on the floor
and lands out of reach

                    ZOEY
               (annoyed)
          Ugh!

ZOEY Stark, 16: throws the sheets from over her head and
comically reaching her entire torso off the bed without
actually getting out of bed. she grabs her phone, and turns
off her alarm.

                    ZOEY
          Im up. I'm up! Yikes!

Zoey lays back in bed on her back and checks her messages.
She responds to a few things then gets up and gets ready for
school. She opens her closet door and picks out a pair of
jeans and tosses them onto her bed. Then she slides some of
the tops over and looks adoringly at one top, she takes it
off the hanger and tosses it onto the bed. She reaches and
picks up a pair of old converse and walks over to her bed
about to get dressed.

She sets the clothes next to each other to see if she likes
the outfit all together and complains.

                    ZOEY
          No, ughh! I have nothing to wear! I
          hate school with a passion.

She goes back into her closet and finds another pair of jeans
with a darker was and tosses them onto the bed,she finds a
long sleeve shirt and tosses it onto the bed as well. Then
when she looks back toward her the closet, she bumps her head
into the closet door.

                    ZOEY
          Agh! Can't just make it through one
          morning without begin a clutz?

INT. LILY'S HOUSE - KITCHEN

LILY Stark, Zoey's mother, 36: is downstairs in the kitchen
making breakfast for her and Zoey. The kitchen has an island
in the middle, and a large silver smart fridge. She grabs the
remote and turns on the tv.

                    REPORTER (O.S.)
          Police are still looking for 15
          year old Amanda Taylor, and her
          brother 8 year old David Taylor.

Lily grabs the remote and turns the volume up, staring at the
screen, shocked and extremely worried.

                    REPORTER (O.S.)
          They've been missing for 2 days and
          were last seen at their home right
          behind me. Police are still looking
          for suspects in their
          disappearance. If you have any
          information please contact the
          number on the screen below.

Lily puts the breakfast on a plate as she continues watching
the news. She gets a piece of paper and a pen and writes down
the number. She shakes her head and looks astonished.

                    LILY
          How can this...to children of all
          people. Why has this world gotten
          so damn cold?

LILY'S HOUSE - ZOEY'S ROOM

Zoey finishes getting dresses as she turns on her tv and sees
the news report on Amanda and David, her expression quickly
changes.

                    ZOEY
          Amanda...

                    REPORTER (O.S.)
          Officer what can you tell us?

                    OFFICER
          No signs of forced entry, which
          leads us to believe it had to have
          been someone that they felt safe
          with.

                    REPORTER (O.S.)
          Any leads on suspect?

                    OFFICER
          At the moment no, but we're
          questioning every friends, and
          families.

Zoey turns off her and stares at it as it goes black, she
looks over a picture of her and Amanda on her wall as has a
flashback to first meeting Amanda.

                                        DISSOLVE TO:

BEGIN FLASHBACK

INT. HIGH SCHOOL - HALLWAY

Zoey is going through her locker looking for her books when
she is approached by Amanda who is starting her first day at
school. Amanda walks up to sorry

                    AMANDA
          Excuse me?

Zoey turns and looks at Amanda.

                    ZOEY
          Yeah?!

Amanda pulls out the school map she got from the front
office.

                    AMANDA
          I'm sorry to bug! I'm new here and
          I'm trying to find "Math 2B", but
          this map they gave me isn't helping
          much, hah.

Zoey laughs as she understands Amanda's situation.

                    ZOEY
          Yea, that map never really helps
          anyone. I have Math 2B too, I'll
          show you where it's at.

Amanda smiles with joy.

                    AMANDA
          Oh my God! Thank you so much! I'm
          Amanda Taylor by the way!

Zoey smiles back at Amanda.

                    ZOEY
          Zoey Star! Nice to meet you!

Zoey walks Amanda to their math class.

                    AMANDA
          So, any helpful tips for the new
          girl on campus?

                    ZOEY
          Umm, not really hah. Just don't eat
          the "Mystery Meat" on Fridays,
          haha.

                    AMANDA
               (laughs)
          Haha, I'll keep that noted hah.

                    ZOEY
          But honestly it's a pretty chill
          school. I mostly stick with my
          friends, you can sit with us if you
          want.

                    AMANDA
          Letting the new girl sit with you?
          I thought it would be more like
          "Mean Girls" hah.

                    ZOEY
          Hah, oh no but we do wear pink on
          Wednesday haha.

Zoey and Amanda share a laugh as they continue walking to
class.

HIGH SCHOOL - HALL MATH 2B

Zoey and Amanda walk into the room and she introduces her to
Mr. Wells, 45.

                    ZOEY
          Mr.Wells! Meet your new student
          Amanda Taylor.

                    AMANDA
          Hi!

                    MR.WELLS
          Ah! Welcome to our school! It's
          free seating so sit where ever you
          like!

                    AMANDA
          Thanks!

                    ZOEY
          There's an empty desk next to me!

Amanda walks over and sits down nexts to Zoey.

                    ZOEY
          This class is really easy. He gives
          you the answers half the time.

                    AMANDA
          Hah, guess this will be easy!

Amanda smiles at Zoey as she reaches into her backpack for
her books.

END FLASHBACK

                                        DISSOLVE TO:
                                        PRESENT

LILY'S HOUSE - ZOEY'S ROOM

Zoey pulls back from flashback as she grabs her backpack off
her bed and heads downstairs.

LILY'S HOUSE - KITCHEN

Lily continues watching the news.

                    REPORTER
          I'm your own opinion do you believe
          this to be the work of the "Cat
          Killer"?

                    OFFICER
          As of right now no, but we're still
          looking into it. Like I said it had
          to have been someone they felt safe
          with.

Zoey comes downstairs and toast her backpack on the couch,
and fixes her hair in the mirror. Then heads into the
kitchen.

                    ZOEY
          Hey mom!

Lily quickly grabs the remote and changes the channel,
looking up at Zoey and smiling.

                    LILY
          Hey sweetie! How'd you sleep?

Zoey walks over and grabs her food off the counter and stars
eating.

                    ZOEY
          Ehh, not too shabby.

                    LILY
          Are you walking to school or is
          Barry picking you up?

                    ZOEY
          Imma walk with Jessica and Hope
          today.

Lily makes a super worries expression, as then hesitatingly
tells her to be careful.

                    LILY
          Be careful, okay? And don't take
          the back roads either.

                    ZOEY
          Of course, we never do mom.

Zoey drinks her juice and glances at the tv. She sees an
Amber Alert for Amanda, she puts the glass down and continues
looking at the tv as it shows pictures of Amanda and David
with the contact number below.

                    ZOEY
               (worried)
          Do you think they'll find them mom?

                    LILY
          As a parent I can only hope so
          baby...I really do..

The doorbell rings, and Zoey gets up and goes answers it.

                    ZOEY
          I got it.

Zoey opens the door and sees her friends JESSICA Jonas, 16:
and HOPE Chang, 15: at her front door.

                    JESSICA
          Hey, you ready?!

                    ZOEY
          Yea, let me grab my bag.

Zoey runs over to the couch and grabs her bag, while Jessica
and Hope wave and say "Hi" to Lily.

                    JESSICA/HOPE
          Hey, Mrs. Stark!

Lily smiles and waves back as she walks towards the door.

                    LILY
          Hi, girls! How are you?

                    HOPE
          Pretty good I guess.

                    LILY
          That's good!

Zoey hugs her mom and heads out the front door.

                    ZOEY
          Bye mom! See ya later!

                    LILY
          Be careful baby I love you!

                    ZOEY
          Love you too!

Lily stands in the doorway outside watching Zoey, Jessica and
Hope walk out of the yard and onto the sidewalk going to
school. She smiles and walks back inside as she closes the
door.

EXT. NEIGHBORHOOD STREET

Zoey, Jessica and Hope are all walking heading to school.

                    JESSICA
          Hey, did you finish that assignment
          from yesterday?

                    ZOEY
          Yeah, it's in my bag.

As Zoey reaches into her bag, she sees police cars driving
the streets. Zoey pulls out the paper and hands it to Jessica
as they all watch the police cars.

                    HOPE
          This is so unreal. Did you hear
          that they think Chad did it?

                    ZOEY
          Chad wouldn't do something like
          that! He loved Amanda.

                    JESSICA
          I don't know Zoey, as a wise man
          once said "There's always some
          bullshit reason to kill your
          girlfriend"

                    HOPE
          You need to stop watching those
          "Lifetime Movies". Zoey has a point
          Chad loved that girl more than
          anything.

Jessica puts the assignment in her purse as she makes a
comment.

                    JESSICA
          Only when she's naked.

Zoey snaps at Jessica.

                    ZOEY
          Really?! Amanda is missing and your
          begin petty?

Jessica winks at Zoey and smiles.

                    HOPE
          You can at least act worried.

Jessica rolls her eyes at Hope's comment.

                    JESSICA
          Anyway, since we're on the topic of
          "Amanda". I heard the "Cat Killer"
          got them.

Hope rolls her eyes at Jessica's comment.

                    HOPE
          That's not even funny Jess! Amanda
          and David are missing, don't joke
          about stuff like that!

                    JESSICA
          Take that stick out your ass Hope.
          I'm just saying what I heard on the
          news.

                    ZOEY
          Who's the "Cat Killer"?!

Jessica and Hope both stare at Zoey.

                    ZOEY
          What?!

                    HOPE
          "The Nanny Killed"?

Zoey shrugs her shoulders.

                    JESSICA
          She's the babysitter who killed the
          kids she watched and sometimes the
          parents.

Zoey's eyes widen in fear.

                    ZOEY
          What?!

                    HOPE
          You haven't heard about her?

                    ZOEY
          No! This is my first time! Do they
          know where she is?!

                    JESSICA
          Apparently not, she could be
          anywhere.

                    ZOEY
          You think she could be here?

                    JESSICA
          For Amanda and David I hope not.
          Well maybe just David, heh.

As the girls keep walking they hear a car horn behind them.
They all turn around and see BARRY Miller, 18: pulling up
next to them, he stops the car.

                    BARRY
          Hey, Zoey! You guys want a ride?

Zoey looks at Jessica and Hope.

                    ZOEY
          Yeah?

                    HOPE
          Saves us time!

Jessica and Hope get in the backseat while Zoey sits in the
front with Barry.

INT. BARRY'S CAR

                    BARRY
          You guys hear anything about
          Amanda?

Zoey looks out the window.

                    ZOEY
          No.

                    BARRY
          You guys think she's okay?

                    HOPE
          We hope so, she doesn't deserve
          this.

                    JESSICA
          I'm sure they'll find her.

                    ZOEY
              (worried)
          I hope so.

Barry notices how sad all the girls are and turns on his
radio and starts singing.

                    BARRY
              (singing)
          20 nights in the ice is a long
          time! When there's hostiles on a
          hill!

Barry points at Zoey.

                    BARRY
          Come on Zoey!

Zoey looks away from the window and smiles shyly, trying to
stay sad about what she's worried about.

                    ZOEY
              (singing)
          Its not about what you want. You
          just gotta walk your walk!

Barry points to Jessica and Hope. They smile and sing along.

                    JESSICA/HOPE
               (singing)
          20 nights in the ice is a long
          time, when there's hostiles on a
          hill!

Barry continues singing while still focused on driving.

                    BARRY
               (singing)
          I wish I wasn't so dang sweet, so
          dang sweet! I wish I wasn't so dang
          sweet!

                    HOPE
               (singing)
          You are like cinnamon!

                    BARRY
               (singing)
          WHOA!!!

They all join in together and sing.

                    ALL
               (singing)
          20 nights in the ice is a long
          time, when there's hostiles on the
          hill!!

They continue to drive down the street singing. As they
continue on, they pass by a house with police officers in
front of it. They hardly notice as they are focused on their
song. The officers walk up to the house.

EXT. NEIGHBORHOOD HOUSE

The officer gather around the front door, and cock their guns
back in position to bust down the door. They signal to each
other: the man in front is the one who will knock. He knocks
on the door.

                    OFFICER 1
          Police, open up!

They wait for a response before kicking the door open.

                    OFFICER 1
          Do it!

The first officer steps back as the next two officers kick in
the door. Immediately inside, there is a trail of blood from
the living room to the back rooms. They slowly walk in with
their guns ready.

                    OFFICER 1
          Stay close!

They slowly walk towards the hall and the blood trails leads
into two different rooms. He signals his men to take the left
room while he takes the right and to kick the doors down on
the count of 3.

                    OFFICER 1
          1....2....3!!

They kick both the doors in and sees the dead bodies of
Amanda and David Taylor in the beds. The officer radios in
what they found.

                    OFFICER 1
          Sir...we found them, but...damn it.

Amanda is found dead on the bed with two stab wounds and her
middle finger cut off, and her brother David is found with
his throat sliced almost to the bone.

EXT. HIGH SCHOOL - PARKING LOT - DAY

Barry parks his car near the back. They all get out of the
car grab their stuff and start walking towards campus.

                    ZOEY
          Oh, Barry can you babysit tomorrow?

                    BARRY
          Umm, yea sure. Why is your mom
          going somewhere?

                    ZOEY
          She has a meeting in TAMPA and
          won't be back for 3 days.

                    BARRY
          Yeah, sure! Just let me know what
          time!

SEBASTIAN Harrison, 17: runs through to the parking lot to
Barry.

                    SEBASTIAN
          Yooo!! Barry!!

                    BARRY
          Wassup, my man!

                    SEBASTIAN
          Please tell me you studied for this
          quiz?!

                    BARRY
          You need my notes huh?

                    SEBASTIAN
          What?! No, I'm offended you would
          think that!

Barry laughs as he takes the notes out of his backpack and
gives them to Sebastian.

                    BARRY
               (laughing)
          Hah, yea okay bitch.

                    SEBASTIAN
          This is why I love you man! Saved
          my ass yet again!

                    JESSICA
          God, no wonder your single, so
          unreliable hah.

                    SEBASTIAN
          Hey, I'll have you know I be
          turning down chick left and right!

                    ZOEY
          Your two chick are your "left" and
          "right"!

They all laugh at Zoey's comment to Sebastian.

                    SEBASTIAN
          You've been hanging around Barry
          too much.

Barr smile and grabs around her shuffles squeezing Zoey, she
grunts and smiles as she pushes him off laughing.

                    BARRY
          She's the little sister I've always
          wanted hah.
               (To Zoey)
          Oh, are you gonna need a ride home?

                    ZOEY
          No, I gotta stay after and finish a
          project.

                    BARRY
          Alright see you guys at lunch!

Barry and Sebastian walk towards the football field.

                    HOPE
          You have like the hottest
          babysitter ever Zo. Like Tapatio
          hot Haha.

                    ZOEY
          Oh my God, Hope! Haha.

                    HOPE
          I mean it's true! Haha

They all giggle and talk about Hopes a comment as the walk
into the building.

INT. HIGH SCHOOL - HALLWAY

Zoey, Jessica and Hope walk to their lockers. Their lockers
are all next to each other.

                    ZOEY
          Oh, Hope do you still have my math
          book?

                    HOPE
          Yeah, here!

Hope grabs Zoey's math book out her locker and hands it to
her.

                    ZOEY
          Thank you!

Zoey puts her book in her locker as she stares at Amanda's
locker. Jessica gets a text from her mom.

                    JESSICA
          Aw, man.

                    ZOEY
          What's wrong?

                    JESSICA
          My moms going out tonight again.

                    ZOEY
          Isn't that the 3rd night in a row?

                    JESSICA
          My mom likes dick more than
          parenting apparently.

                    ZOEY
          Eww, Jessica gross!

                    JESSICA
          Haha, but at least this time she
          hired a babysitter instead of
          leaving home alone.

                    ZOEY
          A babysitter?

                    JESSICA
          Relax it's not the "Cat Killer"
          haha. We hired her last week. She's
          good.

Jessica looks to her left and turns back getting Zoey's
attention.

                    JESSICA
          Look who's here!

Zoey looks and sees CHAD McCALL, 16 walking toward his
locker. All the students stare at him as she walks through
the halls. Chad turns his head and sees Zoey as he walks to
his locker, she smiles and waves at him, he nods his head and
keeps walking.

                    HOPE
          Poor guy. I hope he's okay.

                    JESSICA
          He's a big boy. I'm sure he's fine.

Hope rolls her eyes at Jessica.

                    HOPE
          Can you at least pretend to care
          about Amanda?

                    JESSICA
          I can try, doesn't mean I will.

Jessica wink at Hope and smiles. Zoey shakes her head at
Jessica and Hope as looks over at Chad when everyone phones
begins to off. Zoey looks around at the other students as
they check their phones.

                    ZOEY
          What's going on?! Is it another
          amber alert for Amanda?!

Hope eyes widen as she expresses a heartbroken expression.

                    HOPE
          They found Amanda dead...

Zoey's eyes widen as he checks her phone along the rest of
the student. Chad's mouth drops open as he hurries to check
his phone as well.

                    ZOEY
          Amanda no...

Zoey looks over at Chad as sees him covering his mouth as he
begins to breakdown, he punches his locker and storms out of
the hall in a tearful rage over Amanda.

                    JESSICA
          S-she's really dead...

Zoey looks back at her phone and zones out on the picture of
Amanda as WE PAN OFF OF the phone screen.

EXT. OUTSIDE NEIGHBORHOOD HOUSE - DAY

Police cars and ambulances are parked outside of the house
with caution tape all around and a blockage of policemen to
keep people and reporters back. Detective JAMES, 46: arrives
to the scene and is rushed by reports.

                    REPORTER 1
          Detective James? Do you think this
          is the work of The Cat Killer?

James ignores the reporter and keeps walking.

                    REPORTER 2
          Are the police doing anything to
          insure safety?!

James keeps walking pass the reports and reaches the front
door where a officer is waiting for him.

                    OFFICER 1
          James!

                    JAMES
          What the hell happened?

                         OFFICER 1
          We'll it seems that the killer
          brought them here after kidnapping
          them.

                         JAMES
          Why kill them in someone else's
          home? Who called it in?

                         OFFICER 1
          A Jane Doe called it in sir said
          they saw strange activities going
          on.

                         JAMES
          A Jane Doe huh?

                         OFFICER 1
          It's seems that they were already
          dead before begin brought here.

                         JAMES
          You check records on who owns the
          house?

                         OFFICER 1
          Of course sir, it belongs to a Mr.
          And Mrs. Smith. They were last seen
          last weekend, they were going on
          vacation.

                         JAMES
          Okay, so where the hell are they
          now?

The office takes Jame over to the Haryana opens the door.

NEIGHBORHOOD HOUSE - GARAGE

The officer points to the blue car that Amanda and David were
killed in. James facial expression quickly changes as he
knows who's car that is, he covers his nose with a rag he
keeps in his pocket and walks over to the car. The front
doors are already opened, and James sees the dead bodies of
Mr. And Mrs. Smiths sitting in the front seat.

                         JAMES
          What the fuck...

                         OFFICER 1
          They never made it to the airport.

James looks into the backseat of the car from the front,
which is covered in blood.

                    JAMES
          It's her.. she's here.

                    OFFICER 1
          The Cat Killer?

                    JAMES
          Nancy fucking James.

                    OFFICER 1
          How do you know it's her, sir?

                    JAMES
          You said Amanda's finger was
          missing in your report right?

                    OFFICER 1
          Yes, sir.

The officer hands James the evidence bag with a bloody note
inside of it. James takes the bag and looks at the note, as
he looks back at the car giving the note back.

                    JAMES
          Heather Travis, 16 years old, went
          missing in Dallas 5 months ago.
          They found her 2 days later dead
          with her middle finger cut off and
          a note saying "I told that little
          bitch to respect her elders."

James turns to the office.

                    JAMES
          Which means she's hunt again.

James walks around the car looking inside of it for more
clues. He strokes his chin as she tries to figure it out.

                    JAMES
          We're gonna get you this time
          bitch..

INT. HIGH SCHOOL - MAIN OFFICE

The principal has called a grief meeting for all the
students. Zoey, Jessica and Hope all sit together, when Barry
and Sebastian approach them.

                         BARRY
               Hey, you guy's okay?!

                         ZOEY
               Yea, we're fine..just shocked...

Hope has tears steaming down her cheek as Jessica tries to
comfort her.

                         JESSICA
               Let it out.

                         HOPE
                    (through tears)
               I still can't believe they're
               dead...this just doesn't seem real.

Jessica looks at Barry.

                         JESSICA
               Did they say how they died?

Sebastian chimes in.

                         SEBASTIAN
               Nothing on their deaths yet but the
               media is already saying it's that
               "Nanny Killer".

Zoey and Jessica both look at each other as Barry hits
Sebastian on his shoulder.

                         BARRY
               The Nanny Killer? Come on man don't
               scare them like that.

Zoey looks at Barry desperately for answers for she sees him
as an older brother.

                         ZOEY
               You don't think it's her?

Barry leans against the wall and puts his hand to his face,
thinking.

                         BARRY
               I think it was some sick fucking
               person, not some Nanny Killer.

Jessica looks up away from her phone at everyone.

                    JESSICA
          Oh shit! They found the bodies of
          Mr and Mrs Smith dead in a blue
          sedan parked inside their garage.

Zoey looks even more sad.

                    ZOEY
          What?! Mrs. Smith used to make me
          fresh cookies...

Jessica glances sideways as Zoey, awkwardly trying to think
of something to say in such a difficult time.

                    JESSICA
          Yea, we'll not anymore.

Zoey scrunches up her face.

                    ZOEY
          This is really fucked up..

Everyone looks at Zoey and is surprised she said a swear
word. Barry's eyes widen as he snickers and leans closer to
Zoey and sits next to here, scooting everyone over.

                    BARRY
               (chuckles)
          Did you just say "Fucked"?

Zoey blushes as looks at Barry, she slightly chuckles, but
still on her already-sad emotions.

                    ZOEY
          What?? It seemed like a good time
          to say it. leave me alone haha!

                    SEBASTIAN
          Hah, Zoey said her first big girl
          word aww.

He leans in towards Zoey again, teasing her and trying to get
her to smile and take her mind off the issue at hand. Zoey
smiles all the way this time and flips off Sebastian.

                    ZOEY
          Bite me!

                    SEBASTIAN
          Damn! So sassy!

                    ZOEY
          Oh Barry, I could use that ride
          home now.

                         BARRY
              I gotchu! Just meet me by my car
              after you're done.

Zoey smiles, feeling better and comforted.

                         ZOEY
              Thank you!

The desk assistant opens the door allowing Chad to leave, he
looks up and sees Zoey and starts walking. Zoey jumps up to
go talk to him.

                         ZOEY
              Chad -

Chad cuts her off

                         CHAD
                    (heartbroken)
              Don't Zoey... just don't.

Chad puts his hood up as he leaves the office. Zoey watches
him leave with a sad expression in her face. The Desk
Assistant looks at Hope and signals her to come in. Hope
stands up and wipes off her tears from her face.

                         HOPE
              Here I go.

Hope walks into the office and closes the door. Zoey watches
after her and then looks at Barry.

                         ZOEY
              What does this all seem like
              something out of a bad scary movie?

                         BARRY
              It's all a movie. Just ONE big
              movie, only you don't get to pick
              your genre. The genre picks you.

Zoey nods her head in agreement as she rest her head on
Barry's shoulder as she stares at the missing person poster
of Amanda.

                                        SLOW FADE OUT

EXT. HIGH SCHOOL - PARKING LOT

Zoey is waiting with Jessica in the parking lot for her mom,
as they notice police cars parked along the school.

                    JESSICA
          Crazy isn't it?

Zoey stares off into space.

                    ZOEY
     Yea...

                    JESSICA
     You okay, Zo?

Zoey continues staring off into space but answers Jessica.

                    ZOEY
     Yea, yea. I'm fine...I'm just-

Zoey takes a deep sigh.

                    ZOEY
          I'm just trying to wrap my head
          around all of this, ya know? I
          mean, how does this even happen?!

                    JESSICA
          I know, but honestly I never really
          liked Amanda.

                    ZOEY
          Jessica!

                    JESSICA
          What? I'm just begin real. You and
          Hope are the only people I would
          shed a tear for. I mean it's sad
          but I'm not heartbroken about it.

Zoey looks shocked.

                    ZOEY
          I thought you two were friends?

Jessica kicks a rock away.

                    JESSICA
          Until she stole my boyfriend from
          me...

                    ZOEY
          Right...I'm sorry, Jess.

                    JESSICA
          It's okay... I would say karma's a
          bitch, but-

                         ZOEY
              That would make you the bitch?

Jessica nods absent-mindendly, but then realizes Zoey said
another bad work. She playfully pushes Zoey while laughing.

                        JESSICA
              Zoey?! Two bad words in one day! I
              like it, haha!

Zoey smiles and laughs as Jessica as she playfully pushes her
back. BETTY Jonas, Mother of Jessica, 36: arrives at the
school to pick up Jessica. She pulls in front of Zoey and
Jessica.

                        JESSICA
              Alright Zoey! See you tomorrow!

                         ZOEY
              Sounds like a plan!

Zoey and Jessica share a emotional hug before she leaves.

                        JESSICA
              Love you Zoey!

                         ZOEY
              Love you too, Jessica!

Jessica gets into the car as Zoey says hi to her mom.

                         ZOEY
              My Mrs. Jonas!

                         BETTY
              Hi Zoey! Do you need a ride home?

                         ZOEY
              No, it's okay. Barry's gonna take
              me home.

                         BETTY
              Alright, you be safe sweetheart!

                         ZOEY
              I will!

Betty and Jessica drive off. As Zoey walks over Barry's car
and sees him waiting for her.

                         BARRY
              You ready, champ?

                    ZOEY
          I guess, so.

Zoey and Barry both get into the car and drive off, heading
home.

INT. POLICE STATION - CRIME LAB

James is waiting on the autopsy reports on Amanda and David.
The two morticians pull the bodies of Amanda and David out to
show James.

                    JAMES
          Watchu got for me?

The morticians show James the body of Amanda and David.

                    MORTICIAN 1
          Amanda died from blood loss. She
          was stabbed in the lower abdomen,
          followed by another stab wound
          straight through her heart. Her
          middle finger was broken before
          begin cut off.

                    JAMES
          Killed her slowly and watches her
          die? Typical Nancy James M.O.

                    MORTICIAN 1
          Pretty much.

                    MORTICIAN 2
          As for David he was dead long
          before Amanda. His throat was
          sliced almost to the bone.

                    JAMES
          She killed David first cause he was
          the youngest, and then killed
          Amanda? Somethings off.

                    MORTICIAN 1
          We also found blood on Amanda's
          hands which was her brothers.
          Meaning she tries to stop the
          bleeding at some point.

                    MORTICIAN 2
          But wait there's more.

The mortician gives James the blood lab reports.

                    MORTICIAN 2
          The blood in the backseat of the
          car wasn't Mr. And Mrs Smiths. It
          was Amanda's blood.

                    JAMES
          Amanda's?

James puts the file on the table and walks back and forth
rubbing his hands through his hair.

                    JAMES
          She kills David, then takes Amanda
          to the car and finishes her off
          there? We're missing something,
          this doesn't add up.

James gets a call on his phone.

                    JAMES
          This is James?

The two mortician's look at each other.

                    JAMES
          On my way up now!

James hangs up the phone.

                    JAMES
          We found her phone!

EXT. OUTSIDE ZOEY HOUSE - EVENING

Barry stops in front of Zoey's house and puts the car in
park.

                    ZOEY
          Thanks for the ride.

                    BARRY
          Of course! Oh, what time do you
          need to be over tomorrow?

                    ZOEY
          Oh right! I forgot to ask, sorry.
          I'll let you know later tonight.

                    BARRY
          Gotcha!

Zoey opens the door and gets out of the car and walks towards
her front door.

ZOEY
Bye, Barry!!!

BARRY
Later X.S! Be safe!

Barry waits for Zoey to get inside her house before driving off. She reaches her front door and goes inside and shuts the door behind her. Barry smiles knowing she's safe as he drives off.

INT. LILY'S HOUSE - LIVING ROOM

Zoey tosses her backpack on the counter and calls out for her mom.

ZOEY
Mom, I'm home!

Zoey waits for a response as she walks into the kitchen.

LILY'S HOUSE - KITCHEN

Zoey walks to the fridge and sees a note on the door from her mom "Have to stay late at the office. I'll be home at 11. Dinner is in the oven". She puts the note down and walks over to the oven

ZOEY
What did you leave me mother?

Zoey opens the oven seeing her mom left pizza, she grabs the pizza box out the oven and takes a slice and eats it as she walks back to the living room, and turns on the tv.

LILY'S HOUSE - LIVING ROOM

Zoey is flicking through the channels and starts watching "SUPERNATURAL". She sits back on the eating her pizza while watching Supernatural, when I gets cut to an emergency broadcast.

REPORTER
Today is truly a tragic day, only
hours ago 15 year old Amanda Taylor
and her 8 years old brother David
Taylor were found dead this
afternoon in the home of Mr And
Mrs. Smith.
(MORE)

                    REPORTER (CONT'D)
          After further investigation police
          have came to the conclusion that
          this is the work of the "Cat
          Killer" the infamous Nanny serial
          killer who is responsible for
          missing children in at leas 5
          different states. Police have been
          chasing this serial killer for the
          last 5 years and fear that she is
          now lurking in our peaceful small
          town-

Zoey picks up the remote and quickly turns the tv off. She
stares as the screen goes dark, she rubs the back of her neck
sill not believe what's happening. Her entire mood killed by
the broadcast, another reminder of the reality of things.

                    ZOEY
          The Cat Killer....

INT. POLICE STATION - EVIDENCE ROOM

James arrives in the room and walks over to his partner GAL
Gomez, 33: she hands him a pair of gloves to put on.

                    GAL
          Hey, there you are.

                    JAMES
          Anything?

Gal shows James the text message.

                    GAL
          She lured her outside to the car.

                    JAMES
          What?!

James grabs the phone and reads the messages.

                    GAL
          She made Amanda think she was
          already in the house. And that
          there was an FBI agent outside her
          house.

                    JAMES
          She tricked her into running right
          into her trap? Guess that explains
          why her blood was in the backseat
          of the car...fuck.

                    GAL
          That's not all, she was watching
          Amanda through a teddy bear she had
          in her room.

                    JAMES
          A teddy bear?

James turn to the other officer in the room.

                    JAMES
          Did you guys find a bear in
          Amanda's room?

                    OFFICER
          Yes, I'll go get it.

The officer leave to the back of the room to find the bear.
James turns back to Gal.

                    GAL
          What's the game plan?

James rubs his face.

                    JAMES
          I have no idea, this bitch has
          managed to escape us every time,
          and each time the body counts get
          higher.

Gal looks at James and sees he's stressing over this case as
the the officer returns empty handed. James looks confused.

                    GAL
          Where's the bear?

                    OFFICER
          Umm, it's gone, sir.

                    GAL
          What do you mean it's gone?

James and Gal both stare at the Officer with a furious look
in their eyes.

                    OFFICER
          It's not back there. The lockers
          empty.

                    JAMES
               (angry)
          Its a fucking teddy bear how does
          it disappear?!

INT. BETTY'S HOUSE - JESSICA'S ROOM - EVENING

Jessica has a generic teenage girl room with posters of boy
bands and her favorite celebrities. Her bed is next to the
window. Jessica is laying down on her bed doing homework when
her mom knocks on her door.

                    JESSICA
          It's open!

Betty opens the door holding a teddy bear that was left in
front of the door with a note.

                    BETTY
          I think this is for you!

Jessica sits up on her bed as her moms hands her the teddy
bear.

                    JESSICA
          A teddy bear?

                    BETTY
          Seems like someone has a crush on
          you baby.

Jessica smiles at the bear.

                    BETTY
          Oh, the babysitter will be here
          around 8s

                    JESSICA
          Okay mom.

                    BETTY
          I love you baby! See you when I get
          back.

Betty leaves Jessica's room and closes the door behind her.

                    JESSICA
          This is really cute.

Jessica continues smiling at the teddy bear, unaware that
someone is watching her from the hidden camera hidden inside.
ZOOME IN on the teddy bear.

INT. INSIDE THE CAMERA

With black surrounding the screen, live, Jessica is smiling
at the teddy bear, placing it at the foot of her bed and goes
back to laying down on her stomach as she continues to do her
homework.

INT. ZOEY'S HOUSE - LIVING ROOM - NIGHT

Zoey is asleep on the couch when she is woken up to her phone
ringing. She rolls over and yawns a she searches for her
phone, she moves the pillows and finds her phones, and sees
is Jessica calling.

                    ZOEY
               (half asleep)
          Yeah?

                    JESSICA
               (phone)
          Watchu doing?!

                    ZOEY
          Waking up from a nap what about
          you?

INT. BETTY'S HOUSE - JESSICA'S ROOM

Jessica has her phone on speaker with Zoey while she paints
her toe nails.

                    JESSICA
          Nothing much, just painting my toe
          nails, waiting for this babysitter
          to get her.

                    ZOEY
               (phone)
          What time is she's supposed to be
          there?

                    JESSICA
          My mom said around 8.

ZOEY'S HOUSE - KITCHEN

Zoey gets up and goes into the kitchen while still talking to
Jessica, she looks over at the clock on the fridge door.

                    ZOEY
          It's past 8.

                    JESSICA
               (phone)
          My mom probably told her the wrong
          time or something.

                    ZOEY
          Did you hear what the police are
          saying?

BETTY'S HOUSE - JESSICA'S ROOM

Jessica continues painting her nails.

                    JESSICA
          You mean about the "Cat Killer"?

                    ZOEY
               (phone)
          Yea, do you think thinks it's
          actually her?

Jessica stops painting her nails.

                    JESSICA
          I don't know Zoey, but at least we
          know it wasn't Chad.

                    ZOEY
               (phone)
          You're horrible!

Jessica gets a text message, she checks the message "Hey
running late! I'll be there soon"

                    ZOEY
               (phone)
          Who texted you?

                    JESSICA
          The sitter.

LILY'S HOUSE - KITCHEN

Zoey puts the phone on speaker as she opens the fridge, while
still talking to Jessica. She grabs a side out she fridge and
closes the door. Zoey a cup off the rack.

                    ZOEY
          Why does the sitter have your
          number?

                    JESSICA
               (phone)
          Cause it's 2016 hah. Guess my mom
          gave it to her after what happened
          to Amanda, or maybe it's the Cat
          Killer Hah.

Zoey spills the soda all over her hand as she sets it on the
counter. She flicks her hand to get the soda off.

                    ZOEY
          Can you not joke about that right
          now, Jess?

                    JESSICA
               (phone)
          Oh come on Zoey! lighten up.

BETTY'S HOUSE - JESSICA'S ROOM

Jessica has her feet on top of her desk to dry her nails as
she talks to Zoey stills

                    ZOEY
               (phone)
          This is something serious. Amanda
          and David are dead!

Jessica rolls her eyes.

                    JESSICA
          Okay! I'm sorry it was bad joke.

Someone rings the doorbell. Jessica checks her toes quickly
and drops her feet and get up.

                    JESSICA
          Think my sitters here. I'll call
          you later.

                    ZOEY
          Okay, bye.

Jessica's hangs up the call and get off her bed, heading
downstairs.

INT. BETTY'S HOUSE - LIVING ROOM

Jessica arrives downstairs and opens her front door and
doesn't see anyone. She looks confused, she looks around one
more time before closing the font door.

Jessica walks into the kitchen and grabs herself a bottle of
water. She take out her phone and starts taking selfies when
someone rings the doorbell again.

                    JESSICA
               (annoyed)
          Ugh, I'm so not in the mood for
          this.

She walks towards the front door. She opens it and sees the
babysitter.

                    NACNY
          Hi, I'm your sitter! You must be
          Jessica!

INT. LILY'S HOUSE - ZOEY'S ROOM

Zoey is in her room sitting at her desk looking at videos on
her laptop. She gets a text message from Jessica, she pauses
the video and reads the text "I think my sitter is the Cat
Killer!". Zoey rolls her eyes at Jessica's text as she
replies back "You're not funny, Jess." She sends the message,
and goes back to watching her video.

                    ZOEY
          Oh, Team Four Star is back?!

Jessica sends another text. She looks at her phone and reads
it "I'm not joking! My sitter is acting hella weird! I keep
hearing noises from my kitchen". Zoey tries to calm down
Jessica "Relax you're just paranoid. She's probably just
making something to eat, you'll be fine."

INT. BETTY'S HOUSE - JESSICA'S ROOM

Jessica is sitting on her bed with her door lock texting Zoey
"I'm serious Zoey." She replies when someone rings the
doorbell. Jessica waits to see if the sitter is gonna answer
it.

                    JESSICA
          Someone's at the door!

Jessica waits for a response as the doorbell rings again. She
gets up out of bed and heads downstairs to answer the door.

BETTY'S HOUSE - LIVING ROOM

Jessica makes it downstairs and doesn't see the sitter
anywhere, she looks astound confused.

                         JESSICA
                    Where'd she go?

Jessica walks to the door and opens it. A young women is
standing in the front porch in front of the door, smiling.
She seems a little disoriented, but excited to babysit. One
of her canvas tote bag handles fall off her shoulder and her
planner almost falls out, but she quickly catches it and
shoves it back in.

                         BABYSITTER
                    Sorry, I'm late! I tried texting
                    you, but I don't think you got it.

Jessica's eyes widen as she becomes scared and confused.

                         JESSICA
                    Wait? You texted me?!

The babysitter glances back and forth, a little confused as
well.

                         BABYSITTER
                    Yea, you're Jessica right?

Jessica looks over her shoulder quickly, realizing the person
in her house isn't the babysitter.

                         BABYSITTER
                    Is everything okay?!

Nancy appears on screen and steps directly behind the
babysitter. She wraps her arms around the sitter from behind
and covers her mouth as she slices her throat, smiling
gleefully at Jessica from over the babysitter's shoulder. She
scrunches her nose and her smile widens even as she pushes
the sitters body on top of Jessica. Jessica falls down with
the dead sitter on top of her. She screams in terror as the
blood splashes onto her face, as she tries to push the body
off her. Jessica's clothes are covered in blood and she slips
on the giant puddle of blood on the floor.

                         JESSICA
                      (screaming)
                    Oh God!

Nancy closes the front door as she slides past Jessica
staring down at her while she continues holding her knife.

                         NANCY
                    Heh, aww poor thing. Do you need a
                    towel? Haha!

Jessica manages to push the body off her as she begins to
crawl away from Nancy towards the kitchen down the hall.

                    JESSICA
               (crying)
          Y-y-you're..

Nancy stops and holds her hand with the knife out as of to
taunt Jessica with the idea that she cold easily stab her,
while also making it look similar to a handshake.

                    NANCY
          The Cat Killer, nice to meet you!

Jessica pauses for a second, looks shocked, and then quickly
runs into the kitchen. She looks both ways into the kitchen
searching for something to defend herself with.

BETTY'S HOUSE - KITCHEN

Jessica runs around and slams drawers open very quickly
pushes the drawer's content around, trying to find a knife or
anything. Jessica angrily slams one of the drawers shut.

                    JESSICA
          Fuck!

                    NANCY
          Looking for something?

Nancy stops in the entrance to the kitchen and holds up a bag
filled with knives she tools from the kitchen. Jessica cries
as she keeps her distance from Nancy.

                    JESSICA
               (crying)
          You're the one who killed Amanda
          and David aren't you?

                    NANCY
          Where they friends of yours? I'm
          sorry, but don't worry you'll see
          them again real soon.

                    JESSICA
          What do you want?!

Nancy scoffs as she rolls her eyes and takes a threatening
step toward Jessica.

                    NANCY
          Im so tired of that fucking
          question!
                    (MORE)

                    NANCY (CONT'D)
          "what do you want?", "Why are you
          doing this?". For once I just want
          a kid that doesn't whine.

Tears continue streaming down Jessica's face as she looks at
Nancy.

                    JESSICA
               (crying)
          You're not gonna get away with
          this...

                    NANCY
          Hah, oh really? And are you gonna
          stop me? I'd love to see that.

Nancy slams the bag of knifes on the counter to scare
Jessica, and smoothly takes the sharpest one out. Jessica
tries to make a run for it out of the kitchen, but is grabbed
and slammed hard against the wall causing her head to bleed
as she is thrown to the floor.

Jessica holds her head as she groans in pain while crying out
for her mom.

                    JESSICA
               (crying, groans in pain)
          Mom...

Nancy stands behind Jessica as she tries to crawl away. Nancy
grabs and flips Jessica over on her back and stares into her
eyes with a psychotic grin on her face as she runs the knife
across Jessica's face. Nancy slices a small cut into
Jessica's cheek as she screams in pain.

                    NANCY
          You're gonna die now sweetie!

Nancy pulls back the knife about to stab Jessica, she is
kicked in the stomach and stumbles back as she drops the
knife. Jessica quickly gets up and runs upstairs, as Nancy
does a light chuckle.

                    NANCY
          Oh! I'm gonna enjoy killing you!!

BETTY'S HOUSE - JESSICA'S ROOM

Jessica runs into her room and locks the door. She searches
for her phone to call for help. She panics and tosses things
off her bed and dresser looking for her phone.

                    JESSICA
          Fuck! Where is it?! Where the fuck
          it?!

Jessica looks under her bed and finally finds it. She tries
to unlock it with her thumbprint, but it doesn't work due to
all the blood on her hands. She finally unlocks it the code
and calls Zoey, dropping it while it's ringing and quickly
catches it.

INT. LILY'S HOUSE - ZOEY'S ROOM

Jessica name appears on her phone, she picks it casually and
answers.

                    ZOEY
          He-

Jessica cuts her off.

                    JESSICA
               (crying)
          She's here Zoey!!! She's trying to
          kill me!!'

Zoey's laid-back expression quickly changes to fear.

                    ZOEY
          What are you talking? Who's trying
          to kill you!

BETTY'S HOUSE - JESSICA'S ROOM

Jessica tries to keep quiet so that Nancy won't hear her, but
also us trying to talk through her sobs.

                    JESSICA
               (sobbing)
          The fucking Cat Killer! She just
          killed the babysitter, and now
          she's trying to kill me!! Zoey
          please help me I don't wanna die!!

LILY'S HOUSE - ZOEY'S ROOM

                    ZOEY
               (worries)
          Okay, okay! I'm on my way! I'll
          call the police! Stay in your room
          and block your door! okay?

BETTY'S HOUSE - JESSICA'S ROOM

                    JESSICA
                  (please)
            Hurry Zoey Please!!

Jessica hangs up the call as she put the back of her chair
against the door, and sits down against the bottom of her
bed, holding her knees in fear, clutching her phone.

LILY'S HOUSE - ZOEY'S ROOM

Zoey texts Barry to meet her at Jessica's house. Then dials
911 as she grabs her jacket and rushes downstairs

                    ZOEY
            Hello? My friend is begin attacked
            by the Cat Killer she needs help!
            Her name is Jessica Jonas she lives
            on 117 Elm St. Please hurry!

INT. POLICE STATION - MAIN HALL

James and Gal are at their desk when they get a call about a
home invasion at Jessica's house.

                    OFFICER
            Sir! A call just came in! It's her!
            She's at 177 Elm St!

                    JAMES
            Elm St?

                    GAL
            That's a 10 minute drive. 5 if we
            haul ass!

                    JAMES
            Let's go! Be on the lookout
                  (Into the radio)
            Dispatching all units. Code 10-31

James and a Gal run to their car parked outside.

EXT. POLICE STATION - CONTINUOUS

James and Gal get into the police car and turn on the sirens.

                    GAL
            Think it's really her?!

                    JAMES
          I hope not...for that kids shake.

James pulls out of the station's parking lot and heads toward
the house.

INT. BETTY'S HOUSE - JESSICA'S ROOM

Jessica remains sitting down in her room, holding her knees.
The door is lock as she waits for Zoey to come help her. Then
the door nob starts jiggling back and forth. Jessica starts
to panic and cry.

                    JESSICA
               (crying)
          LEAVE ME ALONE YOU BITCH!!

Nancy begins breaking down the door by kicking it. Jessica
moves into the corner of the room the fear of death looming
over her.

                    NANCY
          Here's Nancy!

Nancy breaks the door down and walks briskly toward Jessica.
In one fair swoop, she leans forward,and picks up off the
ground by her hair. She throws Jessica into her mirror
shattering the glass. Nancy then slams Jessica's head on the
dresser, hard. She then drops Jessica to the floor. Jessica
reaches for a piece of glass on the floor and stab Nancy in
the leg.

Nancy kick Jessica in the face and pulls out the piece of
glass out.

                    NANCY
          Look at you! Haha, we got a
          fighter!

She stabs Jessica in the back 3 times, causing her to cough
up blood. Nancy stands up and starts laughing as she moves
her hair outta her face. Jessica continues coughing up blood
and crying.

                    JESSICA
               (weakly)
          Zoey....

Nancy turns Jessica over on her back and grabs her face as
she continues to stab Jessica in the stomach and chest.

EXT. OUTSIDE JESSICA'S HOUSE

Zoey arrives at Jessica's seeing Barry waiting by his car for her.

                    BARRY
          Yo! What happened I got your text?!

                    ZOEY
          Did you go inside yet?

                    BARRY
          No, I was waiting for you! Zoey
          what's going on?!

Zoey takes out her phone and calls Jessica as she looks at the house.

                    ZOEY
          Come on pick up!

INT. BETTY'S HOUSE - JESSICA'S ROOM

Jessica is half dead on her floor with a thick pool of blood covering her floor, and blood spatter all over her bed and walls. Jessica slowly turns her head and looks at her phone seeing it's Zoey calling as one tear rolls down her bloody face. Nancy grabs Jessica's phone and looks out her bedroom window and sees Zoey and Barry in the front yard.

                    NANCY
          More friends of yours? We'll lets
          not keep them waiting.

EXT. OUTSIDE JESSICA'S HOUSE

Zoey slams her fist down at her side while ending the call with the other hand.

                    ZOEY
          She's not answering I'm going in!

Barry grabs Zoey's arm as he hears the police sirens approaching.

                    BARRY
          Whoa! Zoey wait the police are on
          there way!

                    ZOEY
          Let me g-

Nancy throws Jessica's body through her window into the front yard in front of Barry and Zoey. Zoey and Barry's eyes both widen as they see Jessica's dead body on the ground. Zoey tries to run to her but Barry hold her and covers her eyes.

                    ZOEY
               (furiously crying)
          LET ME GO!! LET ME GO BARRY!!

Zoey breakdown in Barry's arm crying in sorrow. James and Gal arrive along with the other officers to Jessica's house too late. Nancy glances down smiling at the chaos. Just as quick as she appeared, she disappears back into the room. James and Gal get out and draw their guns.

                    JAMES
          EVERYONE IN THE HOUSE NOW! FIND
          THAT BITCH!

The officer all rush into the house to search for Nancy. James looks over at Barry and Zoey.

                    GAL
          Do we question them?

James looks over at Jessica's body.

                    JAMES
          Give'em a minute.

The officers come back out.

                    OFFICER
          We found another body, female
          probably mid 20's but no sign of
          Nancy.

                    GAL
          Are you fucking serious? Fuck!

Gal kicks the trash can knocks it over. James like sullen.

                    JAMES
               (to himself)
          Nancy James is the devil himself.

EXT. OUTSIDE JESSICA'S HOUSE - CONTINUOUS

Officers arrive blocking off Jessica's house, while Barry and Zoey are sitting in the curb in front of the house. Zoey lifts her head as they wheel Jessica's covered body away. Betty returns home seeing the blockage around her house and quickly runs over to the front yard.

                    BETTY
               (crying)
          JESSICA!!

The officer tries to stop Betty from seeing the body.

                    OFFICER
          Ma' you can't go in there!

                    BETTY
          Thats my daughter!

Betty pushes pass the officer and runs over to Jessica's body
on the stretcher and breakdown crying.

                    BETTY
               (crying)
          No!!!!!! Not my baby!!! JESSICA!!!

Zoey and Barry watch as Betty has a breakdown over Jessica.
Gal approaches Betty and takes her away from the body
allowing them to take her inside the ambulance as Gal walks
Betty over to it also.

                    BARRY
          I can't even begin to imagine how
          she feels right now.

Hope comes running over to Zoey.

                    HOPE
          Zoey!

Zoey looks up and sees Hope, she quickly gets up and hugs
Hope as they both start crying.

                    HOPE
               (crying)
          Why Jessica!?

                    ZOEY
               (crying)
          I don't know Hope...I really
          don't...

James and Gal approach Barry and Zoey

                    JAMES
          I'm detective James and this is my
          partner Gal. We were wondering if
          you could answer a few questions.

                    BARRY
          About?

                    JAMES
          Did you know the victim?

                    ZOEY
          She was our friend.

                    GAL
          Did she make contact with you
          before hand?

Zoey sniffles and tears start to form again. She wipes her
face.

                    ZOEY
          Umm yea, she said that her sitter
          was acting weird, but I thought she
          was just joking like she always
          does...then like 20 minutes later
          she calls me crying saying "She's
          here! The Cat Killer is here"...if
          only I listened to her before...
          she would be alive right now...

Zoey breakdown crying and walks away.

                    BARRY
          Go help zoey.

Hope goes to comfort Zoey, while Barry continues talking to
James and Gal.

                    BARRY
          It's really her isn't it? The Nanny
          Killer?

                    JAMES
          I'm afraid so, kid.

Lily pulls up to the house and jumps out of her car running
over to Zoey, hugging her.

                    LILY
          Oh my god Zoey!

                    ZOEY
          She's dead mom....Jessica's dead...
          I couldn't help her...

Zoey grabs her mother tightly as she keeps crying.

                    LILY
          It's not your fault baby. Let's go
          home.

Lily and Zoey walk back to the car, while Barry stays and talks to the cops with Hope. Zoey gets in the car and leans her head on the window wiping away her tears as they drive past the ambulance. Jessica's body is lit up from the lights outside. The light hits Zoey face and reflects her tears and illuminate me the sorrow in her eyes as they drive away.

INT. BETTY'S HOUSE - JESSICA'S ROOM - THE NEXT DAY

James and Gal are working with the other officers to find clues or anything to help them find Nancy. James walks over to the dresser and looks at the door.

                    JAMES
          She was in the corner..

Gal walks over to James.

                    GAL
          She came in, grabbed her and threw
          her into the mirror.

James walks over to the mirror.

                    JAMES
          She falls down and tries to crawl
          away.

James squats down and sees a piece of glass under the bed, he reaches underneath the bed and grabs the broken piece of glass with blood on it.

                    JAMES
          Bingo!

                    GAL
          Watchu got?

He pulls the glass out and looks at it noticing it has blood on it.

                    JAMES
          Our first piece of evidence!

James puts the glass into a evidence bag and seals it closes, he hands it to the other officer.

                    GAL
          Get this to the lab now!

The officer takes the bag and leave as James walks over to the window, staring at the blood spot in the front yard. He looks at the area from that spot.

                    JAMES
          She saw them..

                    GAL
          What?

James turns around looking at Gal, while pointing at the
blood spot.

                    JAMES
          She was standing right here when
          she threw Jessica. She saw them
          outside.

Gal walks over next to James and looks at the spot too.

                    GAL
          She saw Zoey.

James and Gal look at each with a worried look.

                    JAMES
          She saw her next hunt...

James looks back out the broken widow staring at the blood
once again furrowing his eyebrows in thought.

INT. LILY'S HOUSE - ZOEY'S ROOM

Zoey is laying in her bed underneath the sheets looking at
all the pictures of her and Jessica. She stops at a picture
of them taken 3 days agin and smiles at how happy they all
were. She wipes her face as tears roll down her cheek.

                    ZOEY
          I miss you, Jess...I'm so sorry...

Lily knocks on the door as she walks in the room to check
Zoey. She sees Zoey under the covers, and walks over and sits
down on the bed with her.

                    LILY
          How are you holding up baby...

Zoey doesn't respond to her mother.

                    LILY
          Zoey...I know what you're doing
          through honey..

                    ZOEY
          Did you watch your best friend come
          flying through her second floor
          window?

                    LILY
          No...

Zoey removes the covers off her face and looks at her mother.

                    ZOEY
          Then how can you know what I'm
          feeling mom...how?

                    LILY
          A mother can feel her daughters
          pain baby..

Lily reaches out and puts her hand on Zoey's shoulder.

                    LILY
          They'll catch whoever did this to
          her baby.

                    ZOEY
          It was the Cat Killer mom...
          they'll never catch me. She's not
          done hunting.

Zoey pulls the covers back over her face.

                    ZOEY
          I wanna be left alone mom...please.

Lily expresses a heartbroken look on her face as she gets up
and walks toward the door. She looks back at Zoey as she
closes the door. Zoey cries softly under the covers as she
grips the sheets in rage, she throws the sheets off her and
gets up and gets dressed.

EXT. OUTSIDE JESSICA'S HOUSE

James is leaning on the car smoking a cigarette when Gal
approaches him.

                    GAL
          Better slow down. Those will kill
          you before this case does , ha.

James chuckles.

                    JAMES
          You sound like my ex wife, hah.

                    GAL
          Hah, how you holding up?

                    JAMES
          Like shit. The longer that bitch is
          out the there, the more people she
          kill. Nancy James isn't your
          typical serial killer, she a
          fucking hunter! Just when you think
          you got her bam! You're dead.

James takes another puff of his cigarette.

                    GAL
          The reports came back on that blue
          sedan.

James takes a few sigh.

                    GAL
          Turns it wasn't even their. They
          had a 97' Chevy impala, but you
          already knew that didn't you.

James looks at Gal.

                    GAL
          Was that blue sedan your old
          partner's?

James takes another puff as he flicks the cigarette away and
answers Gals.

                    JAMES
          Yea, she went missing 5 months ago
          in Dallas during the Heather case.

                    GAL
          What happened?

                    JAMES
          We were out there to lend an extra
          hand on the case since we had more
          experience. I was at the office
          with the other officers going over
          the clues, while she out on watch
          duty with 4 other officers at
          Heathers house.

                    GAL
          What went wrong?

                    JAMES
          Hell even I don't know. I called to
          get an update and just got radio
          silence then I heard screaming and
          gunshots. I instantly called it and
          had all our troops at Heather's
          houses, and when we got their
          Heather and my partner were gone
          and all our officers were dead. We
          found Heather 2 days later dead,
          but never her. I thought to myself
          maybe she got away but after
          finding her car here...I know she's
          dead.

                    GAL
          I'm sorry about what happened to
          your partner James.

                    JAMES
          I am too.

Gal takes out her flask and hands it to James.

                    GAL
          You could use a drink. If what you
          said about Nancy seeing Zoey is
          right, we might in for a long
          night.

James takes the flask and takes a sip.

                    JAMES
          Let's just hope I'm wrong.

INT. HIGH SCHOOL - HALLWAY

Zoey walks into the main hallway toward her locker. She
passes by Hope without saying a word to her.

                    HOPE
          Zoey?

She continues walking to her locker to switch out her books,
but she stops and stares at the memorial for Jessica they
built around Jessica's lockers that was next to hers. She
walks over to it and takes her bracelet off and puts it on
top of her picture and smiles.

                    ZOEY
          You made that for me in 4th grade
          remember?
                    (MORE)

> ZOEY (CONT'D)
> Hah you said...that I could use
> some more color to my outfit haha.

Hope walks up behind Zoey.

> ZOEY
> I'm so sorry I wasn't there sooner
> Jess... I should've listened
> before...

> HOPE
> It's not your fault Zoey. Don't
> beat yourself up. Jessica wouldn't
> want that and you know it.

> ZOEY
> I know...I just didn't wake up
> excepting my best friend to die.

Hope hugs Zoey from behind.

> HOPE
> Neither did I..

The bell rings for the next class.

> ZOEY
> You should get to class.

> HOPE
> You're not going?

> ZOEY
> I don't want people feeling sorry
> for me right now.

> HOPE
> Do you want me to come over later?
> I can bring pizza!

Zoey does a light smile.

> ZOEY
> Yea, sure. Barry's gonna be there
> too.

> HOPE
> Okay, I'll see you later tonight.

Hope hugs Zoey and walks toward her classroom. Zoey stays and
looks at the memorial one more time before leaving. She takes
one of the photo of the three of them off the memorial and
puts it i her backpack. She walks off campus.

EXT. HIGH SCHOOL - PARKING LOT

Zoey walks through the parking lot as she leaves campus. She
puts her headphones in as she starts walking home. Zoey looks
up and sees a strange car parked in front of the s boy. Zoey
turns and cuts through the football field to avoid the car.

Nancy watches Zoey walk home from inside her car as she
begins to follow her. Zoey hops the fence and turns the
corner heading to her house. She get a text from her mom
"Where are you?!". Zoey response to her mom, she continues
walking home and notices the car is following her. She starts
walking faster.

EXT. NEIGHBORHOOD STREET

The car's windows are tinted so dark that you can't see into
them. The car drives past Zoey as she walking in the other
side of the street. Zoey looks at the car as it drives by and
turns down the next street. She stops walking and turns to
take the back way home. She reaches her street and walks past
Jessica's house, noticing all the caution still up. She ducks
under the tape and stand over the blood stain where Jessica
landed. Zoey looks up at the window and replays what happened
in her head.

                                        DISSOLVE TO:

EXT. OUTSIDE JESSICA'S HOUSE - FRONT YARD - FLASHBACK

                    ZOEY
          She's not answering! I'm going in!

Nancy throws Jessica's through the window and she lands on
the pavement in front of Zoey and Barry. Zoey runs over
Jessica's body.

                    ZOEY
               (crying)
          Jessica!!!

Jessi lifts her blood soaked head and looks at Zoey.

                    JESSICA
          Why didn't you help me!?

Zoey stops in her tracks and starts freaking out.

                    JESSICA
          You weren't there for me!

Jessica stands up and walks towards Zoey.

                    JESSICA
                  (yelling)
          WHY DIDN'T YOU HELP ME!!

Zoey starts having a panic attack and turns around and runs
away but bumps into Amanda with blood on her mouth and all
over her cloths. Zoey freaks out even more as stumbles back
and falls down.

                    ZOEY
                  (crying)
          Amanda...

                    AMANDA
                  (yelling)
          WHERE WERE YOU?!

Zoey breaks down in tears.

                    ZOEY
                  (crying)
          Amanda, I'm sorry-

                    AMANDA
                  (yelling)
          I COUNTED ON YOU! YOU WERE MY
          FRIEND! WE'RE DEAD BECAUSE OF YOU!!

Zoey scoots away from Amanda and bumps into Nancy standing
behind her with a knife in her hand. Zoey looks up and sees
Nancy looking down on her.

Nancy raise her knife and brings it down as Zoey snaps out of
her trance and scream.

                                        DISSOLVE TO:
                                        PRESENT

EXT. OUTSIDE JESSICA'S HOUSE - FRONT YARD - FLASHBACK

Zoey starts screaming as James tries to snap her out of her
bad hallucination.

                    JAMES
          Relax Zoey! It's just me!

Zoey realizes it's Detective James and calms down, she looks
around seeing only James. She wipes her face as she stands up
off the ground.

                    ZOEY
          I-I'm sorry... I know I shouldn't
          be here...

                    JAMES
          It's fine I was actually looking
          for you.

                    ZOEY
          I told you everything I know.

Zoey walks past James as he takes a deep sigh.

                    JAMES
          This is about you Zoey.

Zoey stops and turns around and looks at James.

                    ZOEY
          What do you mean?

                    JAMES
          She threw Jessica out her window
          for a reason.

Zoey looks at the broken window and back to the stain.

                    ZOEY
          She saw me, didn't she? The Cat
          Killer?

                    JAMES
          Her name is Nancy James, and I'm
          afraid so.

Zoey begins s to cry.

                    ZOEY
          She's gonna come after me isn't
          she?

                    JAMES
          There's a chance she will. We're
          gonna have officers stationed
          outside your house tonight.

                    ZOEY
          What about my mom?!

                    JAMES
          We've already informed her. She
          knows.

                    ZOEY
          So, I just sit at home and wait to
          see if I get slaughtered or not?

                    JAMES
          She won't get you Zoey! We'll make
          sure of that.

                    ZOEY
          Like you guys made sure she didn't
          get Jessica or Amanda and David? Or
          the other kids she's killed! How
          many more kids have to die before
          you guys actually do your job?!

                    JAMES
          Zoey I understand your frustration
          trust me. We're doing our best!

                    ZOEY
          Protect and serve my ass.

Zoey walks away towards her house. James run his hand through
his hair as he sighs.

                    JAMES
          Can't blame her for being mad.

James turns and stares at the blood spot on the pavement.

                    JAMES
          This is one kid you won't get
          Nancy. I'll make sure of that.

James walks away as WE SLOWLY ZOOM in on the blood spot.

INT. LILY'S HOUSE - LIVING ROOM

Zoey arrives at her home. Lily and Barry are sitting on the
couch waiting for her.

                    LILY
          Zoey!

                    ZOEY
          I'm okay mom. I was at Jessica's
          memorial.

                    LILY
          Did you see Detective James?

Zoey walks over and sits on the couch next to the window.

                    ZOEY
          Yea, he found me at Jessica's
          house.

                    LILY
          Barry are you sure you'll be okay
          with watching Zoey after
          everything?

Barry looks over at Zoey, then back to Lily.

                    BARRY
          Yes, besides we'll have officers
          outside the house. We'll be fine
          Mrs. Stark don't worry.

Lily smiles at Barry.

                    LILY
          Thank you!
               (To Zoey)
          Is Hope still coming over?

                    ZOEY
          Yes, she'll be over at 6.

                    LILY
          Okay.

Lily grabs her bags and kisses Zoey on her forehead.

                    LILY
          I love you baby. I'll see you guys
          later.

                    ZOEY
          I love you too, mom.

                    BARY
          Bye Mrs. Stark.

Lily leaves the house. Barry looks at Zoey.

                    BARRY
          How you holding up?

                    ZOEY
          I'm not glass Barry. Stop treating
          me like I'm gonna break.

                    BARRY
          Sometimes it's okay to break.

                    ZOEY
          Not this time...if I break I die. I
          gotta stay strong for Jess.

Barry rubs Zoey's back

                    BARRY
          Wanna watch some SPN? I know it'll
          make you feel better!

Zoey giggles and turns around.

                    ZOEY
          Which season?

                    BARRY
          The one when Dean becomes a demon?

                    ZOEY
          Season 10!! Is my favorite, yes!!!

Barry grabs the remote and turns on Supernatural, while James
and Gal pull up and park across the street from Zoey's house.
He turns off the car.

EXT. OUTSIDE ZOEY HOUSE - CONTINUOUS

Gal and James are sitting in the car squad car, getting to
keep an eye on the house.

                    GAL
          Think she'll actually show up?

                    JAMES
          Part of me hopes she does, but the
          other half doesn't.

                    GAL
          Let's say we do catch her, then
          what? Shoot on sight?

James lights his cigarette.

                    JAMES
          Basically.

                    GAL
                (chuckles)
          Hm, thought you say that.

                    JAMES
          We need to catch her. I'm letting
          another kid get buried.

                    GAL
          Has anyone ever lived to see her
          face and give a description?

                    JAMES
          No, everyone whoever see's Nancy
          dies. All we know is that she's
          fast and deadly.

                    GAL
          She sounds like story you would
          tell bad kids.

                    JAMES
          I thought that same thing too once.
          Then I lost my partner...

Gal pats James on the shoulder.

                    GAL
          You still have a partner James. I'm
          a tough one, I won't go do so
          easily.

James chuckles.

                    JAMES
          Alright, imma hold you to that.

                    GAL
          If we get through this night, next
          round of drinks are on me.

Gal and James a quick laugh as they see the other two squad
cars arrive and park three houses down from Zoey.

                    GAL
          Guess it's sometime.

James looks over at Zoey's house.

                    JAMES
          Now we wait.

EXT. NEIGHBORHOOD STREET - NIGHT

Hope is walking to Zoey's house holding a box of pizza, she
passes by Amanda's house and sees Chad sitting on the porch
holding a necklace. She walks over to him to see if he's
okay. Chad looks up and sees Hope.

                    CHAD
          Oh, hey Hope.

                         HOPE
              Chad what are you doing here? The
              police still have caution tape up,
              and you really shouldn't be out
              here alone right now.

Chad holds the necklace up and shows Hope.

                         CHAD
              Yea, I know but...I got this for
              our anniversary. She always said "I
              want a necklace with your name on
              it", ya know? And...I'm not be able
              to give it to her...

Chad grips the necklace tightly as he begins to cry. Hope sit
down next to him and tries to comfort him, putting her arm
around his shoulder. A strange car pulls up and parks three
house down across the street.

                         HOPE
              I know it's hard trust me I do, but
              you gotta be strong! Not just for
              you but for Amanda as well. Amanda
              loved you, Chad.

Chad smiles and looks away, wiping the tears from his face.

                         CHAD
              Heh, I know...thank you.

Chad stands up and puts the necklace in front of the door.

                         CHAD
              There you go baby. I love you!

Hope gets up and hugs Chad.

                         HOPE
              I'm sure she loves it!

                         CHAD
              Thank you, Hope!

                         HOPE
              Of course!

Hope steps down off of the porch and grabs the pizza and
waves goodbye to Chad.

                         HOPE
              See you at school!

                    CHAD
          See ya!

Hope leaves from Amanda's house and continues walking to
Zoey's. Nancy is in the car that arrived across the street.
She watches Hope leave, but focuses in on Chad, and follows
him when he starts walking home.

Chad is walking down the street when Nancy pulls up to him.

                    NANCY
          Hey! I'm sorry to bother you, but
          are you Chad?

Chad looks confused as he keeps walking but answers Nancy.

                    CHAD
          Y-yeah, why?

                    NANCY
          I knew it! I'm Amanda's sister
          Stacy. I didn't mean to scare you.

                    CHAD
          I didn't know she had a sister. She
          never mentioned you.

                    NANCY
          Yea, I'm not surprised. We never
          really got along, but when I heard
          what happened to her I flew out
          here...cause that's still my
          sister, ya know?

                    CHAD
          Yeah, i totally understand.

                    NANCY
          So, where you headed?

                    CHAD
          Home I just got done dropping
          something off at Amanda's house.

                    NANCY
          You want ride? I'm headed that way
          anyway! It's not safe walking alone
          at night pulse we can talk more
          about my sister.

                    CHAD
              (nervous)
          I don't know...

                    NANCY
          I totally understand. You don't
          really know me that well, but come
          on it's better than walking alone
          at night right?

Chad thinks about what Nancy said.

                    CHAD
          Yea, I guess you're
          right...especially since there's a
          killer on the loose.

                    NANCY
          See! There's safety in numbers. Hop
          in Chad!

Chad nods in agreement as he walks over to the car and gets
in. Nancy stars driving.

INT. NANCY'S CAR

                    NANCY
          So how long were you and Amanda
          dating?

                    CHAD
          It was gonna be a year today...

                    NANCY
          Shit, I'm sorry, that's fucking
          rough man.

                    CHAD
          Yea, I should've checked on her
          that night I called her, she
          started acting weird. She said I
          already texted her earlier that
          night.

Nancy looks over at Chad and smirks.

                    NANCY
          Really? That is weird.

                    CHAD
          I know right, at first I thought it
          was nothing, but then she hung up
          like something bad was about to
          happen.

Nancy continues to stare at Chad, as she drives past his
house. He turns around and realizes she passed his house.

                    CHAD
          Oh Stacy you passed my house.

Nancy smiles as she continues to drive.

                    NANCY
          I know.

Chad makes a quizzical expression and raises his eyebrows.

                    CHAD
          Are you gonna turn around?

Nancy turns and looks at Chad with a smile on her face.

                    NANCY
          Now where's the fun in that? Heh.

Chad's eyes widen as he begins to freak out.

                    CHAD
              (terrified)
          T-this isn't funny! let me out of
          the car!

Chad tries opening the door, but Nancy grabs her knife and
stabs him in the hands. Chad screams in pain as the blood
starts pouring out of his hands as he continues to bang on
the window trying to break the glass. Then Nancy slams on the
breaks causing Chad to hit the dashboard. His neck snaps and
Nancy lifts up his head, smiling into his face.

                    NANCY
          Tell Amanda I said hi! Haha.

Nancy continues driving through the neighborhood, Smooth
Criminal playing on her car radio softly.

EXT. OUTSIDE ZOEY HOUSE - NIGHT

James and Gal are still parked outside of Zoey's house
keeping an eye out for Nancy. Gal looks down the street and
sees Hope walking towards Zoey's house.

                    GAL
          Stand down it's just her friend.

                    JAMES
          What time is it?

Gal checked her watch.

                    GAL
          6:30pm.

                    JAMES
          Tell Squad Car 1 circle the block
          for anything suspicious.

Gal radios car 1.

                    GAL
          Squad Car 1 circle the perimeter.

                    OFFICER
               (radio)
          10-4 copy.

The first squad car pulls away and begins driving around the
block. Hope walk up to Zoey's door and rings the doorbell.

INT. ZOEY'S HOUSE - LIVING ROOM

Zoey jumps up and answers the door knowing it's Hope.

                    ZOEY
          Hey!

                    HOPE
          Hey! I brought pizza!

Hope walks in and puts the pizza on the table.

                    HOPE
          Hey, Barry!

                    BARY
          Hey Hope. How you doing?

                    HOPE
          I'm holding up I guess haha.

Zoey goes into the kitchen and grabs 3 cups and a bottle of
soda.

                    ZOEY
          Instead of begin sad and mourning
          her death, let's celebrate her
          life.

                    BARRY
          I think she would like that a lot!

Zoey hands them each a cup of soda.

                    ZOEY
          To Jessica! May she Rest In Peace.

                    BARRY/HOPE
          To Jessica!

They all drink.

EXT. OUTSIDE ZOEY HOUSE - CONTINUOUS

James and Gal are waiting for a response from the guest squad
car.

                    JAMES
          It's radio silence for too long.
          See what's taking them.

Gal radios the 1st squad car and waits for a response.

                    GAL
          Team 1 do you copy?

They wait.

                    GAL
          Team 1 do you copy?

Gal and James start to worry.

                    GAL
          What do you wanna do?

James calls the station.

                    JAMES
          This is James I need a location on
          squad car 556.

The dispatch at the station replies.

                    DISPATCH
          Car 556 last known location was at
          117 Elm St.

                    GAL
          That's Jessica's house.

                    JAMES
          That's not good. Stay here, imma go
          check it out.

                    GAL
          No, I'll go! You keep an eye on
          Zoey.

                    JAMES
          Gal-

                    GAL
          Don't worry James.

Gal grabs her gun and flashlight.

                    JAMES
          You be careful, you here me?!

Gal smiles.

                    GAL
          I always am.

Gal gets out of James' car and walking around the block.
James watches her as she walks around the corner.

INT. ZOEY'S HOUSE - LIVING ROOM

Zoey, Barry and Hope are all sitting in the living room
watching Supernatural together repeating the lines.

                    ZOEY
          "Is he speaking in tongues? Are you
          speaking in tongues?"

                    HOPE
          "What?! No, I'm not speaking in
          tongues"

                    BARRY
          "Then what the hell are you?! Cause
          you're not Sammy!"

                    HOPE
          "Guys it's me I swear!"

They all start laughing.

                    BARRY
          We watch this way too much hah.

                    ZOEY
          It's a great show!

                    HOPE
          But can we all agree that the CGU
          is the best movie universe?

                    BARRY
          Oh, hell yeah!! By far!

                    ZOEY
          I enjoyed the Bathtub Game!

                    BARRY
          That's the one that tells Lily's
          backstory right?

                    HOPE
          Yea, that's the first one.

                    BARRY
          That one was dark.

                    ZOEY
          No, Ludus Plus was way darker. How
          could they have killed Dean like
          that!

                    HOPE
          He didn't deserve to die.

                    BARRY
          No, Mary didn't deserve to die
          either.

                    ZOEY
          Oh my god! I cried at that part. I
          was like "NOOOO!! She finally found
          her!"

                    HOPE
          I liked Allison! She was pretty
          badass, she was ready for anything
          lol.

                    BARRY
          Best female lead, since Jamie Lee
          Curtis!

Someone knocks on the door, they all look at each other.

                    HOPE
          Sebastian?

Barry shakes his head no.

> BARRY
> No, he's at practice.

Barry gets up and walks towards the door.

> BARRY
> Who is it?

They all wait for a response, and get another loud knock.
Hope jumps over to Zoey and holds her hand as Barry walks
closer to the door raising his voice.

> BARRY
> (louder)
> I said who is it!!?

Barry slowly reaches for the door and pulls it open with no
hesitation, and sees a teddy bear with a note attached to it.
Barry reaches down and picks up the bear and close the door.

"Sorry for your loss. Jessica was a good girl"

Barry looks at Hope and Zoey confused.

> HOPE
> Who sent it?

Barry checks the note as Zoey walks over and takes the bear
from him.

> BARRY
> Doesn't say..all it says is N.J. Do
> you know an N.J?

> ZOEY
> No, I don't..

Zoey puts the bear in the table as they all stare at it with
a worried look. Zoey looks at Barry.

> ZOEY
> Something doesn't feel right...

EXT. OUTSIDE JESSICA'S HOUSE - FRONT YARD - NIGHT

Gal arrives at Jessica's house and sees the squad car parked
in front, she walks over to it and checks the side. She looks
at the house and sees the front door. Gal draws her gun and
flashlight as she slowly walks towards the door. She pushes
the door open with her gun, and aims her flashlight inside.

> GAL
> Hello? Anyone here?

Gal walks through the house searching for the officers. She
checks the kitchen and sees a trail of blood leading to the
backyard.

JESSICA'S HOUSE - KITCHEN

Gal aims her light at the blood trail on the kitchen floor
and follows it to the backyard.

                    GAL
          Oh shit.

She walks to the back door and opens it and the body of one
the dead officers swings inward knocking her down. She
screams as she grabs her gun and flashlight off the ground
quickly.

                    GAL
          Fuck! Aha..damn it!

She aims the light at the dead officer and sees he was
stabbed in the neck.

                    GAL
          She's definitely here...

Gal hears a noise coming from upstairs. She quickly turns
around and aims her gun and flashlight at the staircase from
the kitchen. She leaves the kitchen walking along the stairs
aiming her gun and flashlight up the stairs. Gal slowly walks
up the steps as she continues to shine her light up the
stairs. She reaches the 2nd floor and begins searching each
room. Gal kicks in the master bedroom door and does a quick
look around, she checks the closet and behind the door.

She walks out of the master bedroom and goes into Jessica's
room. Gal removes the caution tape from the door and pushes
it open with her gun. Gal walks in and sees all the blood all
over the walls and floor.

JESSICA'S HOUSE - JESSICA'S ROOM

As Gal walks into the room Nancy slowly pushes the door
closed from behind. Gal hears the door slowly close and stops
moving, she turns around quickly and Nancy knocks the gun out
of her hand.

                    NANCY
          Hm, I was hoping James would take
          my bait.

                    GAL
          Sorry to disappoint you.

Nancy laughs.

                    NANCY
          It doesn't matter you'll do I
          guess. I'll send him a piece of you
          like the last bitch he was
          partnered with.

Gal rolls up her sleeves, while Nancy pulls out her knife and
throws it back and forth between her hands and smiles at Gal.

                    GAL
          You can try!

                    NANCY
          I'm gonna enjoy gutting you!

Gal swings at Nancy, she ducks and slices her arm. Gal yells
in pain as Nancy licks her knife and smiles at Gal.

                    NANCY
          Heh, what wrong? Does someone need
          a band-aid? Haha!

Gal rushes Nancy knocking we into the wall and causing her to
drop her knife. Nancy brings her hands together and slams
them on Gal's back knocking her to the floor. Gal moans in
pain. Nancy grabs Gal's hair and knees her in the face,
breaking her nose.

                    NANCY
          Haha, how's that?!

Gal wipes the blood from her nose. Nancy cracks her knuckles.

                    GAL
          Is that all you got?

                    NANCY
          Oh yeah?

Nancy swings at Gal and punches her in the stomach and slams
her into the wall. Gal slides down against the wall and kicks
Nancy in the side of her knee, which knocks her down. Gal
gets on top of Nancy and starts punching her.

                    GAL
          You're mines, bitch!

Nancy breaks free and headbutts Gal in the face. Gal screams
in pain.

Nancy grabs her knife and stabs Gal in the cheek, and pushes
her off. Gal holds her face wound as blood pours out of her
mouth. She rolls over onto her knees as blood continues to
pour out of her mouth. Nancy kicks her over onto her back as
she watches the blood pour from her face down onto the floor.

                         NANCY
            I'm getting the sense of deja vu
            right now, hah. Guess all these
            kills are starting to look so much
            alike it's hard to tell anymore
            hah.

Gal looks up at Nancy as blood continues to pours from her
mouth. Nancy squats down and sticks the knife in Gal's side
and leaves it in.

                         NANCY
            I wouldn't touch that, you'll bleed
            out.

Nancy taps Gal on the face as she grabs her radio and call me
James.

INT. JAMES' CAR - CONTINUOUS

James gets a call in the radio.

                         JAMES
            Gal, I was getting worried. What's
            the word?

                         NANCY
                 (radio)
            Hey James it's been a while.

James' eyes widen.

                         JAMES
            Where is she you son of bitch?!

James grips the radio in rage.

                         NANCY
                 (radio)
            She's right here! Alive and...well
            slight alive hah.

                         JAMES
                 (angry)
            You let her go, do you hear me?!

                    NANCY
               (radio)
          Or else what James? Huh?! You
          couldn't stop me last time. Your
          threats are EMPTY!

                    JAMES
          You bit-

                    NANCY
               (radio)
          Well as much as I would love to
          continue our talk, you might wanna
          get her before she bleeds out. Just
          saying haha.

                    JAMES
          I'LL FUCKING KILL YOU I SWEAR TO
          GOD!

                    NANCY
          Catch me first pretty boy!

Nancy turns off the mic. James punches his dashboard.

                    JAMES
          FUCK!!

James starts the car and turns on his siren and drives off.
Zoey, Hope and Barry see the light from inside the house.

They all walk to the window and see the cop car drive away in
a hurry.

                    JAMES
          Don't you fucking die on me Gal!

INT. LILY'S HOUSE - LIVING ROOM - NIGHT

Hope, Zoey and Barry all look at each other.

                    HOPE
               (worried)
          Why is he leaving?!! What's going
          on?!?

                    ZOEY
          Its her...it's the Cat Killer.

Zoey slowly backs away from the window and starts to freak
out. Zoey grabs her arms as she drops her knees and begins to
hyperventilate.

                    ZOEY
               (terrified)
          She's gonna kill me...she's gonna
          kill me just like how she killed
          Jessica!

Zoey starts crying.

                    ZOEY
               (crying)
          Im gonna die...

Barry quickly walks over to Zoey and hugs her.

                    BARRY
          No! You're not Zoey! I'm not
          letting you die!

                    HOPE
          Me either!

Zoey wipes her tears.

                    HOPE
          We're here with you Zoey. We
          couldn't be there for Jessica but
          we can for you... I don't wanna
          lose another friend.

                    BARRY
          You're not dead yet Zoey. Keep
          fighting!

                    ZOEY
          Thank you guys.

WE SLOWLY ZOOM in on the teddy bear on the table as Barry and
Hope hug Zoey.

EXT. OUTSIDE JESSICA'S HOUSE - FRONT YARD

James arrives at Jessica's house, and jumps out of his car.
He quickly runs inside the house, looking for Gal.

                    JAMES
          Gal!!!

INT. JESSICA'S HOUSE - JESSICA'S ROOM

James runs upstairs into Jessica's room, and sees Gal in the
floor in a pool of blood with a knife in her side. James runs
over to Gal and lifts her head trying to stop the bleed.

                    JAMES
          Oh God! Come on Gal hang in there!

The blood from her mouth runs down James' hand as she reaches
out for him.

                    JAMES
          I got you! I got you!

Gal starts choking on her blood, gagging as she tries to
speak. James tries to hold his tears back as he tries to help
Gal.

                    GAL
               (gagging)
          Zo..z..

                    JAMES
          Don't talk! We're gonna get you
          help!

                    GAL
               (gagging)
          W-why did...you leave...

                    JAMES
          I'm not losing someone else I LOVE!

Gal pulls his face closer to her mouth as she gets weaker due
to blood loss.

                    GAL
          Zo..ey...she's... goi-ng...ughh!

Gal's hand falls to the ground as she dies in James' arms.

                    JAMES
               (through tears)
          Gal? Gal?! Hey!! Come on don't you
          fucking die on me!!

James begins to breakdown crying.

                    JAMES
          Gal no!!! SON OF BITCH!!!!

James holds Gal's lifeless body as he continues breaking down
over her death.

INT. ZOEY'S HOUSE - LIVING ROOM

Barry and Hope are still comforting Zoey when she gets a
strange text message. She checks her phone.

                    ZOEY
          "Did you enjoy the view of your
          friends dead body"....What the-

Barry grabs her phone.

                    BARRY
          Who texted you this?

                    ZOEY
          I don't know...

Barry texted the unknown number back saying "Whoever this is,
you better fucking stop texting this number asshole".

                    BARRY
          They should stop.

                    HOPE
          What kind of asshole sends
          something like that?

Zoey gets another message from the unknown number saying
"Tell Barry I'm gonna kill him first right in front of you".

Zoey begins to freak out as she shows Barry the message.

                    BARRY
          Okay, fuck this. I'll be back!

Barry goes outside to the squad car parked by the house.

EXT. OUTSIDE ZOEY HOUSE - FRONT YARD - NIGHT

Barry walks over to the squad car and taps on the window to
get the officers attention.

                    BARRY
          Guys!

Barry tries to look through the window to see if anyone is in
there.

                    BARRY
          What the fuck. Guys!

Barry opens the door and sees the officers dead and one of
their heads fall out of the car in front of Barry. He falls
to the ground screaming in terror as he gets up and quickly
runs back inside.

                    BARRY
          Oh fuck!

INT. ZOEY'S HOUSE - LIVING ROOM

Barry runs back inside the house, and slams the door and locks it. Zoey and Hope jump up from the couch and look worried.

                    ZOEY
               (worried)
          Barry? What's wrong?

                    BARRY
          T-their dead....

Zoey's eyes widen with fear.

                    ZOEY
          What?!

                    BARRY
               (scared)
          Their FUCKING dead, Zoey!

Zoey gets another message from the number. Barry grabs Zoey's phone and reads the message.

                    BARRY
          "Time to play hide and seek! You
          little shits".

Zoey starts to cry.

                    ZOEY
          She's here...

Barry tries to calm them down and Zoey's her phone back.

                    BARRY
          Hey! We're gonna survive! It's 3
          against 1! No one's dying!

                    ZOEY
               (terrified)
          Yes, we are!!! She killed the cops
          and James-

Hope slaps Zoey.

Barry's eye widen as Zoey holds her face and looks at Hope.

                    HOPE
               (firm)
          You need to stop! You act like
          you're the only one who's scared,
          Zoey!
                    (MORE)

                    HOPE (CONT'D)
          Barry and I are both scared too,
          but we have to be strong! What
          would Jessica say?

Zoey continues holding her face as she looks at Hope.

                    HOPE
          We'll get through this TOGETHER!

Zoey smiles as she looks at home, as she gets another text.
She looks at the message.

                    ZOEY
          "Someone will die, Barry, and it'll
          be Hope first, then you"

                    HOPE
          Is she watching us?!

Barry looks over at the teddy bear, and walks over to it and
flips it over and finds an AV port.

                    BARRY
          There's an AV port on this?

                    HOPE
          Why does it have a port!

Zoey's eyes widen as she realizes what it is.

                    ZOEY
          Cause is has a fucking Nanny Cam
          inside..

Barry looks at Zoey and looks back at the bear, and hooks it
up to the tv. Zoey changes the channel from HDMI to AV and it
shows them watching themselves through the bear.

                    HOPE
          Oh my god...

Barry pushes a button on the bear and it shows Amanda's
bedroom. Their eyes widen as they see Amanda crying in
terror.

                    AMANDA
               (video)
          Why are you showing me this?!

They keep watching the video as Amanda runs out of her
bedroom heading towards David's room.

                    ZOEY
          This is how she killed Amanda...

Barry pushes the button again on the bear and it changes to a
video of Jessica's house, and shows her begins killed by
Nancy. Zoey, Hope and Barry all the watch the video.

Zoey covers her mouth and Hope holds her hands close to her
chest as she starts to cry. Barry covers his mouth and nose
with both of his hands.

                    ZOEY
          Jessica....

                    NANCY
               (video)
          Friends of yours? We'll let's not
          keep them waiting.

They watch Nancy grab Jessica and throw her out of the
window. Nancy walks over and grabs the bear, then the video
cuts off and goes to static. Zoey turns off the tv as they
all sit in silence.

Barry looks at Hope and Zoey. Hope starts to cry as Zoey puts
her head down her hair covering her face.

                    BARRY
          Zoey are you okay?

Zoey walks over to the bear and snatches it out of the tv and
slams it on the ground. She starts stomping on it in a
tearful rage.

                    ZOEY
               (crying furiously)
          You fucking bitch! You killed my
          best friend!!

Zoey breaks the bear as she continues to cry, when she gets a
phone call.

                    ZOEY
          Wha-

                    NACNY
               (phone)
          How'd you like my home movie?
          Jessica was an amazing extra haha.

Zoey's eyes widen when she realizes who it is.

                    ZOEY
          You're not gonna away with this!
          YOU BITCH!!!

                    NANCY
                (phone)
            Oh really?

The lights in Zoey's house go off, causing everyone to
scream.

                    NANCY
                (phone)
            Time to play hide and seek! You
            little shits! You better start
            running!

Nancy throws the head of one of the dead officers through the
front window in the living room landing in front of them.
They all look at the head and scream in terror as Barry tells
them to run.

                    BARRY
            Upstairs NOW!!

Barry lead them all upstairs into Zoey's room.

ZOEY'S BEDROOM - CONTINUOUS

Zoey, Barry and Hope all go into her room. Zoey locks the
door as Barry pushes her bed in front of the door.

                    ZOEY
            What are we gonna do?!

Barry looks around Zoey's room for something they can use.

                    BAREY
            We gotta defend ourselves! Find
            something you can use!

Zoey goes into her closet and grabs a box that has a
butterfly knife in it. Barry finds a cane and Hope grabs
pepper spray. Barry looks at Zoey's knife.

                    BARRY
            A butterfly knife?! Where'd you get
            that from?

                    ZOEY
            It was a birthday gift from my mom.

                    BARRY
            You've used a knife before right?

                    ZOEY
            Stab her with the pointy end.

                    BARRY
          Heh, that a girl!

Barry moves the bed as he slowly opens the door and looks
down the hall while Zoey and Hope stand behind him.

                    BARRY
          Okay, stay close to me , if
          anything happens run! Okay?

Hope and Zoey nod their heads in agreement. Barry takes a
deep breath before opening the door.

                    BARRY
          Okay...let's go.

Barry opens the door and leads them into the hallway. They
slowly walk down the hall, looking for signs of Nancy.

ZOEY'S HOUSE - 2ND FLOOR - CONTINUOUS

Barry continues leading Zoey and Hope down the hallway,
stealthily. They are trying to be careful not to get noticed
by Nancy and to be very aware of their surroundings Barry
whispers to remind them to be careful:

                    BARRY
               (whispers)
          Watch yourself guys. She's here
          somewhere...

Hope grabs Zoey's hand tightly in fear. Zoey gasps lightly.

                    HOPE
               (whispers)
          Zoey..

                    ZOEY
               (whisper)
          I know... I'm scared too.

Barry hears footsteps and stops in front of the hall closet,
putting his hand out slightly to stop the girls. He turns
towards them and puts his finger to his mouth.

                    BARRY
               (whispers)
          Did you guys hear that?

Nancy pushes the closet door open from the inside, knocking
Barry to the ground as he drops his cane. Zoey and Hope
stumble backwards and falls to the ground.

Nancy walks out of the closet slightly closing the door as she steps over Barry, and walk towards Zoey and Hope. She flips her hair back with her hand as she manically laugh.

                    NANCY
          Haha, aww did you fall? was my
          Closet Game joke too much for you?

Zoey stands up and holds her butterfly knife pointing it at Nancy, awkwardly. She is overcome with fear with causes her hand to shake uncontrollably.

                    ZOEY
               (scare)
          S-stay back! I'll stab you!!

Nancy smiles as she walks closer to Zoey and Hope.

                    NANCY
          Butter knife? That's a "Boker Plus
          Trainer". I used to have one too
          well I had a "Bear & Son 114" it
          made killing my first child so much
          easier haha.

Zocy and Hope start backing up towards the wall as Nancy gets closer.

                    ZOEY
               (scared/firm)
          I said stay the fuck back!

Nancy stops and smiles at Zoey.

                    NANCY
          You remind me of my first kill
          Zoey.

                    ZOEY
          What?!

                    NANCY
          The fear in your eyes, the "All
          hope is lost" look on your face.
          The feeling of death looming over
          you, hehe. This feels kinda poetic.

Nancy takes a big step toward Zoey, taunting her. Zoey and Hope slightly jump in fear as Nancy tilts her head to the side as she smiles and leans in towards Zoey. She glances at Zoey's knife and then back at Zoey, still smiling. She bites the edge of Zoey's knife with her head tilted. She laughs and gives Zoey a devious look. She lets go of Zoey's knife. Zoey, scared, stands petrified and her eyes widen.

                    ZOEY
          You Zoey... we're the same you and
          I.

Zoey snaps out of her petrified daze.

                    ZOEY
          I'm NOTHING like you!

Nancy smiles and leans her head real close to Zoey's face.

                    ZOEY
          Oh really?

Barry hits Nancy upside the head with cane knocking her to
the ground.

                    BARRY
          Run!!

Zoey and Hope run past Nancy, but Nancy grabs Hope's leg
causing her to trip. She pulls Hope back towards. Hope
shrieks.

                    HOPE
               (terrified)
          ZOEY!!!

Zoey looks back at Hope and grabs Barry's arm.

                    ZOEY
          HOPE!

Nancy wraps her arms around Hope's head and looks at Zoey and
Barry with a smile.

                    NANCY
          That was a lucky hit kid!

                    ZOEY
          LET HER GO!!

Hope tries to break from Nancy hold, but Nancy grabs Hope's
wrist and snaps it. Hope scream in pain.

                    ZOEY
          Hope, NOO!!!

                    NANCY
          You said no one would die right?!

                    ZOEY
               (crying)
          NO! PLEASE! LET HER GO!!

                    NANCY
         Sure.

Nancy breaks Hope's neck as she stares Zoey in the eyes. Zoey
screams. Nancy throws Hopes body into the wall like a rag
doll. Barry tries to pull Zoey away so they can run, Zoey
stands in one spot, petrified.

                    BARRY
         Zoey! Come on! We gotta go!

Barry grabs Zoey's arm and pulls her downstairs. As they
reach the bottom of the stairs, James comes charging in
through the front door, covered in Gals blood with his gun
ready. Barry and Zoey stop and look at home.

ZOEY'S HOUSE - LIVING ROOM - CONTINUOUS

James is standing inside, facing Barry and Zoey who just
stopped running from Nancy.

                    JAMES
         Where is she?!

                    ZOEY
         Upstairs! She killed my friend!

                    JAMES
         You two outside, now! I'll handle
         this!

                    BARRY
         No! She'll kill you too!

                    JAMES
         Then I'll take her with me! OUTSIDE
         NOW!!

James runs upstairs as Barry goes outside. Zoey stays inside
and watches James go upstairs.

                    BARRY
         Zoey!

Zoey grips her knife tighter and starts to cry. She runs
outside with Barry.

ZOEY'S HOUSE - 2ND FLOOR

James arrives upstairs with Nancy sitting next to Hope's dead
holding her head up. James aims his gun at her.

                    NANCY
          James, how'd you been? I'm guessing
          you didn't save your partner in
          time again?

                    JAMES
               (yelling)
          GET THE FUCK UP NOW!!

                    NANCY
          I'll take that as a yes, haha.
               (Looks at Hopes body)
          You hear that Hope? We gotta get up
          haha.

James walks closer to Nancy with his finger in the trigger
ready to shoot.

                    JAMES
          Is this a fucking game to you?!

Nancy takes her hand off her head and sees she's bleeding.
She licks her fingers.

                    NANCY
          I gotta say these kids put up more
          of a fight than Gal did haha.

James shoots Nancy in the shoulder.

                    NANCY
               (in pain)
          Aha-haha! Did that feel good?

James walks over and picks Nancy up, and slams her against
the wall. Nancy groan in pain.

                    NANCY
          At least by me dinner first, James.

                    JAMES
          Shut your fucking mouth!

Nancy shakes her head and laughs.

                    NANCY
          Should've gone for the head James.

Nancy throws her head back and breaks James nose with a
headbutt. James stumbles back holding his nose, yelling in
pain. Nancy runs down the hall as James starts to shoot at
her Zoey and Barry hear the gunshots from the front yard.

James quickly runs after Nancy and follows her downstairs. He reaches downstairs and sees her run into the kitchen, he follows behind her.

ZOEY'S HOUSE - KITCHEN

James has his gun ready looking for Nancy, he searches the kitchen and stops in front of the glass backyard door. Nancy charges at James from within the darkness and tackles his through the glass door and he shots off another rounds

EXT. OUTSIDE ZOEY HOUSE - FRONT YARD

They hear the other shot go off. Zoey tries to run back inside in, but Barry grabs her arm.

                    ZOEY
          Let me go!!!

                    BARRY
          Zoey, I know your mad about Hope
          but this isn't gonna help her! We
          gotta let James-

Zoey pulls away from Barry.

                    ZOEY
          I've lost 3 people I've cared about
          in the span of 3 days! I am not
          leaving until I see her die!

                    BARRY
          Are you listening to yourself?!
          This isn't you!

                    ZOEY
          Are you?! You promised me no one
          would die and look what happened to
          Hope!

Zoey runs back into the house with butterfly knife in her hand.

INT. ZOEY'S HOUSE - 2ND FLOOR

Zoey runs upstairs and sees blood and bullet holes in the wall. She walks over to Hopes body and squats down next to her. She closes her eyes and tries not to cry.

                    ZOEY
          I'm sorry Hope...tell Jessica I
          miss her.

Zoey heads back downstairs into the kitchen, and looks around
for James and Nancy. She walks over the shattered glass on
the floor from the back door and sees drops of blood leading
outside.

ZOEY'S HOUSE - KITCHEN - CONTINUOUS

Zoey stops before the broken glass momentarily, psyching
herself up to fight Nancy.

                    ZOEY
          This is for Hope and Jessica...

She steps through the broken door into the backyard.

EXT. ZOEY'S BACKYARD

Zoey's backyard is a large field with a 12ft foot pool and a
tool shed near the left side of the house. Zoey slowly walks
over to the tool shed following the trail of blood, she
reaches out to open the door, he hand shaking. She swings it
open and sees James dead in the ground.

                    ZOEY
          No!

She runs over to his body and sees he's been stabbed in the
neck. Zoey notices his gun and radio near his body. She
reaches for the radio and tries to call for help as she picks
up the gun. She cocks back the gun and holds down the radio
button.

                    ZOEY
          Hello! I need help! I'm of 227 W.
          Wood Av-

Nancy appears behind Zoey and covers her mouth as she grabs
her and throws her out of the shed onto the ground m. Zoey
hits her head on the ground and starts bleeding. She touches
her head and sees blood on her hand. Zoey groans in pain as
she reaches for the gun, but is kicked in the stomach by
Nancy who takes the gun and throws it by the back door.Zoey
yells in pain.

                    NANCY
          Come on Zoey! Get up!

Zoey tries to crawl away and gets up but is kicked once again in the stomach by Nancy. She holds her stomach as she continues trying to get away.

                    NANCY
          You're mines!

Zoey stabs Nancy in the leg with her knife. Nancy limps away and laughs. Zoey gets up off the ground. Nancy pulls the knife out of her leg and licks her blood off of it. She throws her hair back with her head and laughs at Zoey.

                    NANCY
          I like you Zoey! You're more fun
          than your friends.

Nancy passes Zoey's knife back to her, handle facing Zoey.

                    NANCY
          Pick it up.

Zoey looks down at her knife and then back at Nancy. She slowly reaches down and grabs her knife.

                    NANCY
          There you go Zoey!

                    ZOEY
          Why are you doing this?

Nancy starts walking towards Zoey. Zoey makes her way closer to the pool.

                    NANCY
          I was bored, I like to hunt, you
          we're home? Which one do you like?

Zoey walks closer to the pool as Nancy follows.

                    ZOEY
          You're just killing to kill aren't
          you?

                    NANCY
          What can I say? Something about
          watching the life leave a person's
          body is satisfying for ya know?

Nancy stares at Zoey with a devious look in her eye. Zoey, looking at Nancy, raises one eyebrow and glances off to the side, acknowledging that she's crazy.

                    ZOEY
          No....I don't know.

Zoey stares directly into Nancy's eyes angrily.

                    NANCY
          You're eyes say another story Zoey.
          You wanna kill me for killing your
          friends, huh?

Zoey grips her knife tighter. Nancy laughs at her.

                    NANCY
          You do, huh?

                    ZOEY
          You won't win.
              (Beat)
          Nancy…

Nancy gives Zoey a look for knowing her real name, she
smiles.

                    NANCY
          You know what? Jessica said that
          same thing, so I'll you what I told
          her "Are you gonna stop me?!"

Nancy speed walk towards Zoey and swings her knife at her.
Zoey jumps back, avoiding the blade, as she tries to stab
Nancy. Nancy chuckles at Zoey.

                    NANCY
          You're full of piss and vinegar!
          I'll rip you open and show you your
          guts!!

Nancy swings at Zoey with the knife. Zoey grabs her wrist and
drags her into the pool as she jumps into it herself. They
struggle underwater, trying to gain control of the knife.
Nancy stabs Zoey in the shoulder twice and slices her arm.
Zoey kicks Nancy in the face, and swims quickly back to the
top of the water. She resurfaces, trying to swim back to the
edge of the pool as the pool slowly fills with blood. She
reaches the edge and tries to pull herself out. She slips and
groans.

Nancy rises up behind Zoey, and raises her hand, about to
stab her. Zoey turns her head and looks over her shoulder at
Nancy. She quickly closes her eyes as Nancy gets shot by
Barry, who is standing across the pool. Nancy falls back into
the water. Zoey looks up at Barry. Barry is shaking as he
drops the gun on the ground, looking astonished. He looks
into the pools after Nancy's body falls back in. Then he
notices Zoey again and runs over to her to help her out of
the water.

                    BARRY
          I gotchu Zoey!

Barry helps Zoey up. Zoey is dripping wet with blood and
water. She looks back at Nancy's dead body and then back at
Barry. She wraps her arms around Barry and puts her face into
his chest, crying softly.

                    ZOEY
          I'm sorry...thank you Barry!

Barry hugs her back and grips her shoulder and nods lightly.
They let go of each other and return to the front yard, as
the police arrives.

EXT. OUTSIDE ZOEY HOUSE - FRONT YARD

Zoey and Barry are sitting on the ambulance truck as they
finish patching up Zoey. Lily arrives and runs over to them,
worried. Lily hugs Zoey.

                    LILY
          Oh my God, baby!! I'm so glad your
          okay!

Lily looks over at Barry and hugs him too.

                    LILY
          Thank you for saving her life
          Barry!

                    BARRY
          Just doing my best...just wish I
          could've saved Hope too.

Zoey reaches over and holds Barry's hand.

                    ZOEY
          You did all you could, Barry.

Barry looks at Zoey. Zoey turns her head towards the house
and notices they only pulled out two bodies instead of three.

                    ZOEY
          Where's the third one?

                    EMT
          We only found two bodies my

                    BARRY
          There should be three! What about
          the one in the pool?!

                    EMT
          Wasn't one in there.

Barry and Zoey look at each other as they run to the
backyard.

ZOEY'S BACKYARD

Zoey and Barry stare at the blood filled pool.

                    BARRY
          She got away...

Zoey looks down and sees her butterfly knife on the ground.
She reaches down and picks it up.

                    ZOEY
          For now....she'll be back. I'm the
          hunt that got away.

Barry and Zoey look at each other as the sound of sirens
become louder and the light get brighter. Zoey lays her head
on Barry's shoulder.

                    BARRY
          We'll be ready next time.

Zoey keeps her head on Barry's shoulder as the sirens reach
their loudest.

INT. LILY'S HOUSE - ZOEY'S ROOM - 2 WEEKS LATER

It's been 2 weeks since Zoey fought off Nancy and lived to
tell about of it. She's been taking self-defense classes ever
since, and is skilled with her butterfly knife collection,
which is hanging up on the wall. Her self-defense classes are
listed in an open agenda book on her desk, and she has two
karate gi's hanging in on her closet door. Zoey, 18 years old
now, is sitting on her bed watching tv waiting for Barry to
text her. She turns her head and looks at the picture of her,
Jessica and Hope. She gets up and walks towards it as she
smiles.

                    ZOEY
          Can't believe it's been 2 weeks
          already. I miss you guys everyday.

Zoey rolls up her right sleeve and reveals that tattoo she
has on her wrist in memory of her friends. She rubs it and
smiles, as she gets a call from Barry. She flips onto her
belly on her bed as she answers the call.

                    ZOEY
          Are you outside?

                    BARRY
               (phone)
          Yea, just pulled up!

                    ZOEY
          Okay, I'm coming!

Zoey hangs up the phone and grabs her purse off of her and
walks towards her door. As she begins to leave, she hears an
important broadcast in the television.

                    REPORTER
               (tv)
          It's been 2 weeks since our small
          peaceful community was struck with
          fear after The Cat Killer killed a
          group of teenagers leaving only 16
          year old Zoey Stark and 18 year old
          Barry Miller the soul survivors of
          the "Cat Killing".

Zoey turns around and watches the newscaster.

EXT. OUTSIDE ZOEY HOUSE - FRONT YARD

Barry is parked outside of Zoey's house waiting for her in
the car, he scrolls through his phone as he listen to music.
He sees the news article about him and Zoey.

                    BARRY
          "The Cat Killing Survivors" Cant
          wait till this shit blows over.

He puts his phone down and turns up his radio and starts
singing along to the song.

                    BARRY
               (singing)
          You are like cinnamon. Whoa! 20
          night in the ice is a long time ,
          when theirs hostiles on a hill!

INT. LILY'S HOUSE - ZOEY'S ROOM

Zoey is standing in her room still in a short of trance
facing the tv. She continues watching the news as she sits
down on the edge of her bed.

                    REPORTER
          Within the last two weeks there
          have been reports of missing child
          in at least 3 different states. The
          most recent victim was 17 year old
          Maria Lopez who went missing just 4
          towns over.

Zoey turns off the tv and watches it go black. She heads for
her closet and reaches for her box with her knife in it. She
opens the box showing the knife from that night stained with
Nancy's blood. Zoey takes out the knife and looks at herself
in the mirror

                    ZOEY
          I'm ready for you this time
          Nancy...you'll pay for what you
          did.

POST CREDIT SCENCE

INT. BUSINESS OFFICE - DAY

STEVEN ALLEN, 45 years old is the hiring temp manager for his
company. His office is large with a large window out looking
the city. He has a large oak desk with pens perfectly places
along the edge of his stack of papers. His next appointment
walks into the room, Steven looks up and sees Nancy James, 42
years old with long blonde hair and a nice smile. Steven
motions Nancy to sit a room from him at his desk.

                    STEVEN
          Have a seat.

Nancy walks over in front of his desk and sits down.

                    STEVEN
          I'mma be honest and
          straightforward, if you want this
          job I need you to answer truthfully
          and directly, okay?

Nancy nods her head in agreement.

                    NANCY
          Of course, sir.

Steven looks at Nancy quizzically but continues.

                    STEVEN
          What we're looking for is someone
          who won't flinch at killing them.

Nancy smiles slightly as she remembers her past kills.

                    NANCY
          I can handle that.

Steven doesn't notice her smile, and continues.

                    STEVEN
          A quarter of the job is making sure
          they don't get sick, but other than
          that it's just putting them down.
          You've obviously done that before
          right?

Nancy nods her head and tries to hide her smile.

                    NANCY
          Yes.

Steven glances at Nancy.

                    STEVEN
          Off the record, how do you do it?

Nancy thinks about it for a moment.

                    NANCY
          I look into their eyes and watch
          the light leave. I've done it quite
          a few different ways.

Something about her statement disturbs Steven, as he looks
away and makes a questionable look. He then shrugs slightly
because she was the first candidate who actually seemed fine
with the position. Nancy notices his angst and tries to
reassure him.

                    NACNY
          The younger they are, the easier it
          is, since they don't know what's
          coming next. It's the older ones
          that can sense what you want to do,
          and they'll put up a struggle of
          course.

                    STEVEN
          I'm sure it must be hard.

                    NANCY
          It is, but I'm really good at what
          I do and I'm very discreet.

Steven stands up and Nancy stands up after him. He reaches
over his desk and holds out a firm hand. She shakes his hand
and smiles gleefully.

                    STEVEN
          Well you're a shoe in for the job!
          I'll get back to you by the end of
          the week.

Nancy gives a sideways half smile.

                    NANCY
          Thank you!

Nancy smiles at Steven as she leaves the room. He places her
file in the "Yes" pile. His next interview walks in BRUCE
West, 40: with a beard and tattoos. Steven makes a confused
expression because the paper in front of him indicates that
he is about to be interviewed fir the executive Nanny
position.

                    STEVEN
          You're here for the nanny position?

Bruce laughs as he pulls his beard.

                    BRUCE
              (laughs)
          No, I'm here for the Veterinary
          Position!

Steven's eyes widen at Bruce's response. He immediately
hurries out of his office towards his assistant.

                    STEVEN
          Gwen! That women who was just
          here...what position was she here
          for?

Gwen checks her computer.

                    GWEN
          The Nanny Position. That's Nancy
          James, she comes highly
          recommended.

                    STEVEN
          Nanny Position?!

EXT. OUTSIDE OFFICE BUILDING

Nancy is walking back to her car smiling as she takes off her
blonde wig and throws it in the car through the window. She
unlocks the door and gets in.

INT. NANCY'S CAR

She starts the car and adjust her mirror. She looks at her
lips in the mirror and smiles. She touches the bullet wound
scar on her right shoulder. Nancy reaches into her glove box
and pulls out the blade that she stabbed Zoey with 2 weeks
ago licks it. She laugh manically.

                    NANCY
          Haha, it's hunting season again
          Zoey.

Nancy drives out of the parking lot onto the street and
drives off into the city.

                                        SLOW FADE TO
                                        BLACK

www.ingramcontent.com/pod-product-compliance
Lightning Source LLC
Chambersburg PA
CBHW052112150726
48002CB00006B/2320